THE CHA
JOHNNY VA

Jamie Rix is the son of actors Brian Rix and Elspet Gray. A TV producer in his spare time (Smith and Jones, *KYTV*, Harry Hill), his first children's book, *Grizzly Tales for Gruesome Kids*, was published in 1990 and was the Smarties Book Prize Children's Choice. Since then he has adapted *Grizzly Tales* and his other collections of cautionary tales, *Ghostly Tales for Ghastly Kids*; *Fearsome Tales for Fiendish Kids* and *More Grizzly Tales for Gruesome Kids* into an award-winning animation series on CITV. He has written several other books, including the prequel to this title, *Johnny Casanova, The Unstoppable Sex Machine*; *Free the Whales*; *The Fire in Henry Hooter* and his first picture book *The Last Chocolate Biscuit*. Married with two grown-up sons, he lives in south London.

Books by the same author

Johnny Casanova, The Unstoppable Sex Machine

The Fire in Henry Hooter

For younger readers

Free the Whales

THE CHANGING FACE OF JOHNNY CASANOVA

JAMIE RIX

For Ben and Jack,
inspirations both

First published 1998 by Walker Books Ltd
87 Vauxhall Walk, London SE11 5HJ

This edition published 2002

2 4 6 8 10 9 7 5 3

This book has been typeset in Sabon and Providence

Printed in Great Britain by Cox & Wyman Ltd, Reading, Berkshire

British Library Cataloguing in Publication Data:
a catalogue record for this book is
available from the British Library

ISBN 0-7445-9048-5

CONTENTS

1	Coming of Age	7
2	Choosing Miss Right	16
3	Action Man	28
4	Diabolic Steroids	40
5	A Bit Moody	49
6	In at the Deep End	64
7	The Power of Prayer	88
8	Warm Beer in the Freezer	105
9	Every Wallet has a Silver Lining	125
10	Bosie Spells it Out	130
11	All Change	142
12	Burnt Beans and Frostbite	169
13	Dream On	203
14	The Rave	206
15	The Morning After	233

1
COMING OF AGE

It was the hordes of have-a-go hormones that did it – swirling round my bloodstream like tadpoles in a blender. When I was thirteen, I thought like a boy, I played like a boy and I chased girls like a moth in a light bulb factory. But when I turned fourteen I put away boyly things and became a man.

It happened overnight. My body underwent a major makeover, and I'm not just talking about clumps of hair sprouting in all those sweaty places where my limbs joined, I'm talking about a mental transformation as well. My mind grew up. I didn't have time for giggly girls any more, I wanted women. I wanted a meaningful relationship with a sophisticated chick, a meeting of mature minds, a long kiss with tongues.

A NEW PERSPECTIVE ON GIRLS

At thirteen years, my sexification
Was lacking in discrimination.
Anything what had a dress on
Was my permanent obsession.
But now that I have come of age,
Just fourteen years, but oh so sage,
I'm ready for a grown-up date,
Where couples talk and cogitate.
I don't ask much,
I don't want kids,
I don't want rows with saucepan lids,
I don't want jointly held accounts
Or houses costing vast amounts.
I just want someone cool and chic
Who'll stay with me more than a
week.

(Johnny Casanova – from his new collection of poems, "On The Knee Of Old Age Sits The Travel Rug of Responsibility")

Anyway, I can remember waking up on the morning of my fourteenth birthday and thinking, *This is it. I'm a man now*, and lifting up the duvet to check if I was, which was scary at the time, but turned out to be a risk well worth taking, because what I saw underneath the cotton tent enabled me to go back to school with my head held high. I knew I hadn't dreamed it. I *had* gone to bed butt-naked. I was sleeping pyjamaless; the mark of a real man.

The first day of a new term is always a bind, but the start of this particular Autumn Term filled me with nervous anticipation. Not because I had a new form master, Mr Dibcock, whose shirts had yolk-yellow stains under the armpits that smelled like fried onions, but because I had to look safe when I appeared in the playground. I had to make a dynamic first impression on the new girls.

For once, styling my sacred hair took no time at all. I'd been developing a crusty, rebel, grunge look over the holidays, by letting it grow out and not washing or combing it since 15 July, and rubbing John Innes Potting Compost No.1 into the roots once a week. The fringe hung limply over my eyes like a rack of rats' tails, the sides curled naturally behind my ears after weeks of laborious flicking, and the clump at the back swung greasily over my collar like a racehorse's blanket after a sweaty, five mile chase. If I shook my head, lumps of sebaceous lard sprayed the mirror. I was well pleased. It looked dead nasty.

My facial hair growth was spectacular. I hadn't shaved for four and a half months and people had started to comment on the luxuriance of my straggly goatee beard, a three-haired flow of unkempt wispiness that made me look at least twice my age. Even though it was against school rules I decided to keep it, to make my school mates jealous. Then I undid my top button and tied my school tie in a huge knot by winding the dangly bits round and round about fifty times. When I'd finished, all that was left (apart from the knotted beehive under my chin) was a tiny triangle of tie at the front and a long thin bit at the back, which I stuffed through the buttons of my shirt as carelessly as I could. Then I put on a pair of non-regulation red socks, ripped a small hole in the knee of my trousers with Dad's nail file and tore one of my blazer pockets till it hinged along the bottom seam and flapped down like an Elizabethan codpiece. I looked rebellacious! Much too mature for girls my own age. If the sixteen-year-olds didn't go crazy for me, then my name wasn't Johnny Casanova (which it isn't, it's Worms, but you know what I mean).

I tiptoed downstairs and sneaked out the front door before Mum could see what I looked like. She had a bee in her bonnet about me looking respectable when I went to school and one sight of my co-ordinated grunge look would have had her tidying me up for a week. I was pushing my bike down the front path, when Ginger leapt out from behind the hedge and greeted me with a full-blooded karate chop across my neck.

"Mind the hair, mate!" I winced, straightening my neck with a sharp crack of dislocated bone.

"Got you!" he sniggered. "That hurt, didn't it?"

"I thought you were learning judo," I said grimly.

"We started karate last night," he grinned, ducking and swerving in front of me, before landing a four-knuckle jab in my gut.

"I wish you'd stop doing that," I gasped, "or I'll have to smack you one."

"I'd like to see you try," he crowed.

I'd noticed a change in my best mate since he'd taken up martial arts. He was turning into a more physical, bulging biceps, slab of beefcake type of bloke, ever keen to test the rock-hardness of my six-pack with a surprise punch in the solar plexus. Let's be perfectly frank, he was a mad macho-merchant, and I'd got the cuts and bruises to prove it.

"I *could* duff you up if I wanted," I said, as we cycled side by side down the road, but Ginger just laughed.

"I don't think so, Johnny. Bernard says I'm the best pupil he's ever had."

"Who's Bernard?"

"My teacher."

"Bernard! What sort of name's that for a martial arts expert?"

"He's a plumber."

"Shouldn't he be called something like Blind Old Grasshopper or Enigmatic Mongoose?"

"I'll have you know he's the South Peckham T'ai Chi Champion."

"So he can deep fry prawn balls!" I sniggered. "So what?"

"He believes that, as an urban warrior, I should have a grounding in the entire panoply of Eastern Mysticism."

"Urban warrior! Ginge, you're scared of your own shadow."

"Not any more," he said proudly. "He's helped me to develop an inner strength. T'ai Chi's a way of centring. Watch." He jumped off his bike and performed a slow motion dance on the pavement, wiggling his left hand across his belly and pushing away with his right. "That's called Step Back and Repulse Monkey," he said.

"Very handy if you're mugged in the jungle," I said. "Bernard sounds cracked to me. What else does he do? Step Forward and Put on Strait-jacket?"

"Aha, aha," said Ginger. "My sides ache!"

After that Ginger didn't talk for a bit. I expect he was locked in meditation with his mystic monkey or something. When he did speak, I wished he hadn't, because he made a thorough job of puncturing my new-found confidence.

"Just what in the name of Jarvis have you

come as?" he said. I nearly fell off my bike.

"Slashes and grease are sexy."

"You look like a headbanger."

"This is what the girls like," I informed him.

"No, they don't. Girls like someone normal who they can talk to, not some primeval blob that grunts at them in the tuck shop."

"Since when did you suddenly become an expert?" I bristled. "I haven't exactly noticed passion-wagon loads of pent-up totty beating a path to your door."

"Doesn't bother me."

"Are you gay?" I needled, which really got his goat. It was as if I'd just accused him of loving Radio Two swingle-singing.

"Get stuffed," he said, fetching me a friendly Major Reap in the pelvis.

"So why haven't you got a girlfriend?" I wheezed.

"Who says I haven't?" he challenged. "*You* haven't."

"I have," I lied. "Nearly."

"I've had several offers," said Ginger, "but I'm waiting for a girl I really like."

"Why?" I gawped. "Ginge, don't you know nothing? Girls don't grow on trees. You've got to seize the moment, mate, take the first available train. There may not be another one along ... ever."

Just then, as if sent to test me, the gorgeous girl in the purple uniform, who cycled past us every morning and whom I hadn't yet plucked up the courage to speak to, pulled out of a side street and surfed towards us.

"Here's your chance," said Ginger. "Ask her out."

"What, now?" I prevaricated, as a glimpse of her black tights paralysed my sense of time and space.

"You're the stud," he smiled. It was my fault for opening up the can of worms in the first place. Now I had to eat them.

"I will then," I said. I hadn't felt as nervous as this since Mum caught me looking at a shower catalogue in the bathroom. "Mmworfffgg," I mumbled as Purple flashed past, throwing in a half-hearted wave for good measure when I was sure I was out of her sight.

"Mmworfffgg!" roared Ginger. "What's that? You've got to give it a bit of passion, Johnny." He turned round and demonstrated. "Morning!" he bellowed after the purple princess, who promptly stopped her bike and waved at him.

"Hi, Ginge!" she called and then she went on her way. You've no idea what that felt like; like finding your mum in bed with the milk-man or finding out that your nan's rice pudding, which you'd always thought was home-made, came out of a tin.

"Traitor!" I gasped. "She belongs to me. I'm the one who has sleepless nights over her, not you!"

"She does judo with Bernard," said Ginger. "Did I forget to tell you? We had a close contact tussle on the mat last week. She's a lovely mover."

I'd heard enough. To think that Ginger knew girls and I didn't! What was the world coming to?

ON BEING GRACIOUS IN THE FACE
OF OVERWHELMING PROVOCATION

Finding girls is not a race
I'm glad I've learned this early.
Quantity cannot replace
The luv of just one girly.
Nonetheless...
If girls would only look at me
Instead of ogling Ginger
I'm sure they'd like what they did see.
I hate that red-haired Ninja.

(Johnny Casanova – in league with the
little green worm of jealousy)

2
CHOOSING MISS RIGHT

After Ginger and I had parked our bikes, I strolled around the perimeter of the playground scowling like I was deep in tortured thought. I was trying to ooze adult sophistication, but actually I was fighting a sudden and overwhelming desire to hunt the hotties, which had swamped me on the way to the bike sheds and shot my birthday resolution to pieces. Obviously, if I was ever going to have myself a mature, monogamous relationship with the girl of my dreams, it was going to take a Herculean feat of concentration.

I spotted one new face amongst the old ones. It belonged to a tall boy with short blond hair and acne. I pointed him out to Ginger.

"If I ever look like that—" I said.

"He can't help it," interrupted Ginger.

"Buy a paper bag and shove it over my head," I told him. Suddenly a voice called out

"Johnny!" from over by the toilets.

"Who's that?" Ginger asked.

"Sam Driver," I said. "They're our new neighbours. Mr Driver drives a brown Austin Maxi with fake fur seat covers. Dad loathes them."

"No wonder," said Ginger.

"But Sam's safe," I said, as Sam's curly mop bobbed through the crowd towards us.

"All right?" said Sam.

"All right," I monotoned. "And you?"

"Yeah, good," said Sam. "It's not so bad here."

"This is Ginger."

"Hi."

"It's Sam's first day."

"Are you from up North?" asked Ginger, cocking his ear to Sam's accent.

"Hull," said Sam. "But we left when I was seven. We were living in Weymouth, till Dad got his promotion."

"He's big in incontinence pads," I said. "Head of Sales or something."

"Would you like me to teach you Waza-ari?" asked Ginger obliquely.

"Why?" said Sam.

"Well, if anyone ever took the piss out of your accent," he explained, "you could put them in hospital big time."

"I'll bear it in mind."

"No pressure," added Ginger. "It's your decision."

"You haven't seen any new girls have you?" I asked.

"How would I know?" said Sam. "I'm new here too, aren't I? Got to go. S'later."

"Look," said Ginger, after Sam had gone, "if you want to meet girls, go and meet *them*." He was pointing at a gang of new girls huddled by the water fountain like a flock of frightened sheep in a thunderstorm.

I scoured the group for older talent, for someone to match my advancing years, but they were all turned inwards talking to each other and I couldn't see their faces. Their backs were daunting. It was a shut-out. Then suddenly they all turned round and stared at us staring at them. They were giggling like ponies with hiccups, and covering their faces with their hands, as if the sight of Ginger and I was the funniest thing in the whole universe since Take That's first video.

"Well, go on then," urged Ginger. "Go and speak to them."

Suddenly I didn't feel like meeting the new girls after all. Ever.

"There's too many of them," I hissed. "We're outnumbered. Besides I don't fancy any of them." The truth was, gangs of girls were more scary than a trainload of Millwall supporters. "Anyway, it's not just any old girlfriend I'm looking for. She's got to be the right one."

"That's not what you said earlier on," protested Ginger. "You said I had to take the first girl who came along." My superior laugh was tinged with disdain.

"Ginger," I said, "one day you will learn that love is rarely consistent. Take Napoleon. In-between battles and going mad, he was at it all the time with Josephine, until one night, out of the blue, he suddenly says, 'No. Not tonight, Josephine.' Just imagine that poor woman's confusion. Does he love me or doesn't he? Maybe he doesn't like my new perfume, or maybe he's drunk too much brandy. The truth was he just didn't fancy it. Love was *not* consistent. See?"

"You're just chicken!" snorted Ginger.

"Chicken yourself," I replied.

"I'm not the one who's changed his name to Johnny Casanova, am I? I'm not the one who thinks he's the world's greatest lover." That was one thing I really hated; Ginger telling the truth when it was true.

Suddenly, a tall girl, with long black hair shouted, "What's your name, Shorty?" which had Ginger and I both turning round at the same time. "I mean you," she added, pointing at me. At ME! The cheek of it. I wanted to call her something rude back but, put on the spot, I couldn't think of anything sufficiently cutting, and she *was* twice my size, so I let it pass and said good morning to the Headmistress instead, who flashed me a withering look of disapproval and told me to shave off my bum fluff.

"YOU LOOK LIKE A DANDELION," she boomed.

Thanks, I thought, and you still look like something the cat brought in, but I didn't actually say it, obviously. I had to hide my embarrassment fast, so I slunk over to the fence to examine knotholes. Ginger followed, still milking the "shorty" joke.

"There's a couple of pygmies over there," he sniggered, nudging my elbow and pointing out two lonely figures standing about ten metres away. "They're more your size." I couldn't be seen to duck out of two pick-ups in a row, so I moved in, circling the girls at a distance, like a Great White Shark, while I sussed them out. They were identical twins – as alike as one person split in half by a lightning bolt – which was lucky, because then it wouldn't matter which one fancied me, and they weren't that small. In fact they were quite pretty, in a faded English Rose sort of a way, with bobbed blonde hair framing their ash-white faces. "Come on," said Ginger, shadow-boxing my arm. "There's one each."

"Ow!" I said, as he misjudged another punch and thrombosed my upper arm. "That flippin' hurt, you psycho!"

I followed Ginger over to the twins, making

maximum use of my new hairstyle. By stuffing my hands deep into my trouser pockets I was able to affect an impressive stoop, which rounded my shoulders and pulled my neck down and forward, which in turn caused my hair to flop over the top and dangle lankly over my eyes. Obviously this meant I couldn't see a thing, let alone how the twins were taking to me, but they probably thought I looked dead mean and moody. Ginger didn't bother to look sharp, he just strolled up and said "Hello". Just like that. Cool as a cucumber. He didn't pretend he'd lost something, or make out as if he'd met them before but couldn't remember where, or even try a corny chat-up line, like "Do you fancy coming here often?" Just, "hello", like he knew they were going to warm to him from the off. And strangely, they did. They said "hello", back and the conversation rolled on from there.

"I'm Ginger."

"I'm Daisy and this is my sister, Rosie."

"Are you twins?"

"Yes," they said together. I mean, it wasn't very romantic stuff, but it was highly effective.

"We're both Flowers," they said.

"I can see that," I chipped in, trying to flatter them with wit.

"No, that's our name," said Rosie. "Rosie and Daisy Flower." I felt like a berk, but kept smiling.

"You've got red hair," Daisy said to Ginger.

"Yeah," he replied. "So has my mum." As the conversation progressed, I became acutely aware that I was making zero contribution. I felt like a support band at a rock concert, the one that nobody's interested in.

"Hi, I'm Johnny," I said, trying to rectify the situation. They waited for me to elaborate on this scintillating news. "Er ... Johnny Casanova," I grinned.

"We've got a cousin who looks just like you," said Rosie. "He absolutely hates washing his hair, because the soap stings his eyes."

"So he never does," added Daisy. "Wash his hair, I mean. That's why it's greasy like yours."

I wasn't entirely sure how to take that. It stopped me dead in my tracks. Meanwhile Ginger had started smiling and scratching his ear, and they were smiling back. He must've had a musk tablet in his boxers the way all the girls were suddenly falling in love with him.

"So," I heard him say effortlessly. "Have you always been twins or is it something that just happened one day?" Their sweet, tinkling laughs drove a dagger through my heart and I crept away from this double rejection with all the dignity of a naked rambler accidentally strolling on to the eighteenth green at Gleneagles in front of six thousand spectators.

Where were all the nice new girls – the ones

that fancied *me*? I was beginning to wonder why I'd bothered to come back to school at all. Didn't the new talent know how much charisma they were missing?

All the old faces were still there, worst luck, all except Deborah Smeeton – Little Miss Metalmouth, Cyborg Chops, The Girl with the Bionic Brace – who'd followed me around for the last two years, trying to get me to kiss her. I collared Cecil Simpson, who was playing hopscotch with a group of first years and asked him where she was.

"Hello there, Johnny," he said. "Do you like me?"

"Not much," I mumbled. "Where's Deborah?"

"She's left," he said sadly. "I loved her, Johnny, with all my heart."

"Where did she go?"

"She moved house to be closer to her orthodontist." Cecil looked gutted. I slapped him on the back.

"You'll find another woman," I lied encouragingly.

"I doubt it," he gulped. "I caught eczema in the holidays – at Butlins in Bognor."

"Oh, I am sorry," I said, moving away quickly before I caught it, and bumping into my old girlfriend, Alison Mallinson, who was hiding behind a large and obvious copy of *Brides and Bridesmaids*. That's another thing

I hate; when people try to tell you something without actually telling you something. Her pillar box beau, a jealous brute of a boy with the muscles and IQ of an anaesthetized rhino, who went by the name of Timothy Winchester, grabbed me by the lapels.

"Hands off, Worms!" he boomed. "We're betrothed."

"I hope you'll be very happy," I smiled disingenuously, spitting out a mouthful of Timothy's nose hair. "May all your babies be human. Goodbye." It must have looked like I'd been scared off, but actually something had caught my eye.

Over by the dining hall, a gang of boys were whooping it up. I wandered over to see what the attraction was and stood at the back of the crowd as a pair of upside-down shoes spun past the heads in front of me. I pushed forward to see who they belonged to and walked into a dream. The Goddess Venus was cartwheeling across the concrete. She bounced to her feet, then dropped down gracefully on her haunches and stood on her hands, resting her feet against the wall. I hyperventilated as her short skirt flopped down round her waist. She was magnificent. I had to show her to Ginger. I dragged him away from Daisy and Rosie and shoved his head through the swelling throng.

"Look at that!" I said breathlessly. "I'm in love!"

"Only because you can see her pants," said Ginger.

"Don't spoil it," I said. "She's got lovely pants, I grant you, but she's also beautiful and I bet she's got brains too. How old do you think she is?"

"Fifteen," guessed Ginger.

"At least," I sighed. "She's perfect." The crowd applauded as she flipped over into the crab position and scuttled round the ring.

"Her name's Bosie Cricket and she's here on a Sports Scholarship," said a voice in my ear.

"Well, that's you out of the picture," chortled Ginger.

"I can do sport," I said.

"You can't. Your head's always too full of girls," he said .

"I want her, Ginge. She's so ... flexible."

"She's my best friend," said the voice. That was just what I wanted to hear. I spun round to quiz my unknown source further, only to be confronted by a pair of large ears dripping with cheap gold rings. The girl had long, wet hair slicked back off her face, like she'd flattened it with wallpaper paste, and two ringlets dangling over her eyes. On her arm she had a real loser. Obviously her boyfriend, because *his* hair was a major tragedy too. It was bleached and cut short with one of those ragged, toothy fringes. Outside their shirts they were wearing matching identity chains, which confirmed what I already suspected: their names were Sharon and Darren.

"Pleased to meet you," I said sweetly. "If you're Bosie's best friend, can you introduce me?"

"You can introduce yourself," she said. "She's trying out for the swimming team after school." My reputation was saved. I had found my other half. Now all I had to do was steal a pair of swimming trunks so she could find *me*!

ON ME AND SPORT THUS FAR IN MY LIFE

Whacking balls and stroking leather,
Kissing posts and Arctic weather,
Legs like ice-pops, stiff and blue,
Hands so numb the catch goes through.
Hearty, yomping sporting masters,
Tending broken necks with plasters.
Rinsing down in freezing showers,
Comparing parts for hours and hours.
Why the need to run so quick?
Why cross countries to be sick?
Up till now the only sport,
That has my jaded interest caught,
Is women's hockey on TV,
Watched by girls at Wemb-er-ley.
I dream their screams are all for me.
But now that I've met Bosie,

There's no more time for posey-posey!
It's down the gym and up the beef,
'Cause Casanova's très sportif!

(Johnny Casanova – in training for a five-mile run over rough country ... get it?)

3
ACTION MAN

Stealing the trunks was easy. I waited till the changing room was full and all the boys had their trousers off, and then I got Ginger to call out "Fire!" at the top of his voice. "Leave everything exactly where it is and evacuate the building immediately." Ginger said he nearly shouted, "Evacuate your bowels immediately," which would have rather blown the gaff, but luckily he didn't, and the changing room emptied quicker than a shower full of girls finding peepholes in the tiles. Actually, the ploy scored a double whammy, because it not only got me a pair of trunks for the trial, but also provided the unmissable sight of Timothy Winchester standing in the quad in nothing but his obscenely huge, off-white underpants, while the whole school filed past on their way home, shouting, "Hail, Caesar!"

Timothy screamed blue murder when he

discovered his trunks were missing.

"But I'm the school swimming champion," he wailed at Miss Percival, the swimming teacher.

"Not if you can't find your trunks," she said briskly. She was the only person I knew who could do synchronized swimming without a nose plug, because her nostrils were naturally mean and pinched. "You know the rules. No trunks, no swim."

"But I've shaved my chest for the competition!" blurted the vast, Y-fronted boy, gasping for air like a tuna-fish out of water. The sense of injustice was suffocating him. I judged this to be my moment to approach.

"Excuse me, Miss," I said, raising my hand politely. "While Timothy's looking for his trunks, might I try out for diving?" I couldn't swim for toffee, but falling off a diving-board looked simple enough. Timothy's eyes bulged in their sockets.

"Those are my trunks!" he exploded. "He's wearing my trunks!" He lunged forward like a granny at a Chippendales gig and tried to tear the flimsy material off my nether regions. The pain, as he twisted the lycra and attempted to wrench it through my pelvis, was excruciating.

"Aaaagh!" I screamed. "He's got hold of my ... ooh, aah, urgh! I think I need a doctor, Miss!" But Miss Percival's mouth was locked in an "O" of astonishment, and while she stood by doing nothing, Timothy sat on my head. My throat emitted a strange gurgling noise as my neck was squashed like a squeezebox. My eyes filled with serious tears and I was all for conceding possession of the trunks, when I managed to grab hold of a handful of little black hairs on the back of Timothy's thigh and tore them out. The fighting stopped instantly. Timothy roared with pain and ran out of the changing room clutching his leg, while Miss Percival found her voice at last.

"It's the headmistress for you, Winchester!" she squeaked, as I slipped victorious out to the poolside where my stolen swimwear was ridiculed by the other swimmers. Timothy's trunks had been big on me to start with, but now, after our tug-of-war, they were billowing round my knees like a Sultan's pantaloons.

Just then Bosie appeared in a slinky, black one-piece.

ON LYCRA

Lucky, lucky lycra
Clings where
I would like ta.

(Johnny Casanova – in need of a cold shower, pronto monto)

Her auburn hair was pulled up tightly into a bun, accentuating her lovely bone structure. She walked confidently across the slippery tiles to where we were all standing, drawing her towel gently back and forth across the nape of her neck. I flicked my hair behind my ears and sucked in my cheeks to look cool, then peered intensely out of the window at the sky and pretended I wasn't interested, but really I was watching her reflection in the plate glass, mentally drooling over her catwalk wiggle. She knew *exactly* the effect she had on boys. And I succumbed. My legs turned to jelly and I slipped over the edge into the pool.

The water slapped me round the face like a wet towel and brought me to my senses. Instinctively I struggled towards the surface, but I heard distant laughter and realized I'd made a first-class fool of myself. What should I do? Drowning was the least embarrassing option, but if I topped myself I'd never get to meet her, and I couldn't just sit on the bottom for ever because my lungs were burning. I had to come up and face the music. With my arms flailing I burst out of the water, spluttering and coughing, and grabbed the edge of the pool with one hand, whilst trying to sweep my hair out of my eyes with the other. I lost my grip and plunged back down, only this time I got a mouthful of water which filled my lungs like a fish tank. I was suspended in liquid gelatine, floating in a cave of thundering silence. My limbs moved in slow motion as I tried to wave at the row of distorted heads peering down at me.

"He's drowning!" came the muddled cry, and suddenly there was a second body in the water next to me. Strong hands grabbed my waist, steered me up towards the light and flopped me over the edge like a rag doll. Before I could move, several other hands flipped me over and scraped my shoulder blades across the concrete nipples on the floor tiles as they dragged me to safety, whereupon I realized, with horror, that tearful, fist-raising Miss Percival was preparing to restart my heart with a sternum-smashing punch that she'd learned as a first aid instructor in the army.

"I'm all right," I bubbled, fending off the blow and trying to save face by spluttering, "I meant to do it!" Miss Percival collapsed with nervous relief. Her swimming trials were turning out to be a trial of quite a different sort. "Who pulled me out?" I asked, parting the overhanging crowd as I sat up.

"I did," said my saviour, brushing the water off her long, slender arms. "Hi, I'm Bosie." It was the voice of an angel.

There comes a time in a man's life when he realizes what is important to him. Bosie had just saved my life and I knew I would never be the same again. There was a spontaneous explosion of love in my head and my life's purpose was revealed to me in a sublime vision of tear-jerking clarity. It was Bosie. The gods had spoken. My heart was hers to command for ever. She was my destiny. She was my woman.

"What happened to you?" she asked. Telling the truth would only have made me look a prat.

"I was practising my diving," I faltered, trying to recover poise points by standing up and readjusting the two-man tent round my waist. "It's a new one I just invented. It's a double pike with forward tuck roll and belly flop. I don't think I'll bother with it again."

"It did look rather dangerous," she smiled, wrinkling the freckles on her nose.

"It's meant to. The art is making it look like you've just fallen in," I said, as a stream of water gushed out of my nose and brought half my brain with it. "Sorry," I mumbled, turning away and wiping the snot off my top lip with the back of my hand. Oh God, it was all going horribly wrong! I tried to pretend it had never happened and said conversationally. "So, lovely old swimming! What strokes do you do?"

"All strokes," said Bosie, as Miss Percival blew her whistle and called the trial to order, "but breaststroke's my favourite."

Bosie's breaststroke was heavenly and I couldn't resist a quip as she pulled herself out of the water after winning her race.

"I like breast stroking too," I grinned, boldly.

"So why weren't you racing?" she asked.

"I'm not talking about swimming," I said, raising an eyebrow and giggling attractively, like one of those witty blokes you see on "Blind Date".

"Oh, you mean sex," countered Bosie. Blimey, what a girl! Mentioning the "S" word before she even knew my name! I knew I had to sound like talking dirty was second nature to me, but my voice kept leaping up an octave with excitement and all I could do was yelp like a little lap-dog.

"Do you want to know what my fantasy is?" she whispered in my ear. I nodded my head like a cat-flap in a high wind. "To do a forty-minute snog, without coming up for air." I grunted with a mutual desire for the same. She was so sophisticated. "And I'm looking for a boyfriend right now," she added, bending down in front of me to pick up her towel. "See you..."

"Johnny," I said, finding my ragged voice in the nick of time. "Johnny Casanova. I ... you ... we... Yes?" I was a gibbering wreck. I wanted to go after her, but Miss Percival had just called my name and insisted on seeing what I could do off the high-board. What I did was severe damage to the top of my skull as I entered the water. I thought I'd split it right down the middle like a coconut. My legs jerked forward over my shoulders and I landed smack on my back with a shuddering impact that sent a spray of water six metres into the air. Luckily for me, nobody else wanted to try out for diving after witnessing my painful effort, so Miss Percival offered me a place in the team.

"Only you'll need a new pair of trunks," she said. "In the school colour – green. Our first gala's on Friday. Tell your parents. Thank you all for coming." We were dismissed.

I got dressed in double quick time and rushed out of the changing room to intercept Bosie before she went home. I'd been bold by the pool, but now that it was just us, my brain seized up. I couldn't think what to say. I knew what I wanted to say, which involved pinning down the time and date of a certain forty-minute snog, but she'd have hit me. Suddenly I had a brainwave.

"Silverfish," I said. "Potato-head. Excalibur's biscuits."

"What are you talking about?" she laughed.

"I can't find the words to ask you out," I said, sheepishly. She laughed again. God, I was good. God, she had lovely lips. "So will you?" I panted.

"Maybe," she said. "I always spend Saturday nights in The Freezer," she continued.

"Why don't you come? We could see if we gel."

"In the freezer?" I said. "Isn't that a bit cold?"

"It's a nightclub," she whispered, like I was a dork or something. To tell the truth, I felt I'd got KEVIN stamped across my forehead in non-washable ink.

"Oh, *that* Freezer," I grinned, biting the inside of my cheek to teach my big mouth a lesson. "Sure. I go there all the time." There was a short silence while my lie stood up and announced itself. Then I added, "Will it just be the two of us?"

"No," she said. "All my mates will be there."

"Excellent," I said. "Mates are excellent."

"And Elastic Strawberry are on."

"Groovy," I replied enthusiastically. "Ooh great! Wow, yeah, ktang, ktang, take me to the mountain, they're my favourite! I love strawberries!"

"They're a band."

"Of course they are," I blushed. "I know that. I can't wait to snog with you, Bosie ... *dance* with you, I mean!" I wanted to die. My mouth had developed a death wish of its own. Someone sew it up! But Bosie was laughing. She didn't seem to be offended at all. She just said, "See you," and then she was gone. I could hear her laughing all the way to the bus stop.

LUV – ADULT STYLE

Oh Bosie,
You're rosie,
You're peaches and cream.
You're ice in a bucket
With Oysters Supreme.
You're sin in a swimsuit,
Your voice can melt fire,
Your lips drop sweet pearls,
Like sweet notes from a lyre.
I wonder if you're at home
Thinking of me?
Do our hearts beat as one yet
In synchronicity?
I bloody hope so.

(Johnny Casanova – in torment till I hear her voice again)

As I pushed my bike across the playground and swung my leg over the crossbar, my brain was befuddled by Bosie's bewitching brown eyes and I couldn't get her miniskirt out of my head either. I lost control of the handlebars and smashed into Sam, who'd been in detention for flicking pencils on to the fire escape.

"You'll never guess what's just happened to me," I gushed.

"You've just gone blind," Sam said sourly, rubbing the bruises.

"Yeah, in a way," I said. "Blinded by love. I've got a real girlfriend." Sam didn't seem impressed. "Her name's Bosie."

"Bosie Cricket?"

"How did you know that?"

"Because she was at my last school. She's got a reputation as a collector of boyfriends. Apparently, she's got more scalps under her bed than Geronimo."

I didn't like the sound of that. My hair was sacred.

"She doesn't really ... you know ... use a tomahawk, does she?"

"I believe so," said Sam. "On those who disappoint."

"Disappoint?" I gulped. Flashes of failed Freezer-talk flitted through my brain. "Do you think I'll disappoint her?" Sam grinned like this was some sort of game.

"Well, it's only a rumour, you understand, but I've heard she only gets turned on by really big men."

"And you think I'm short?"

"Not short," answered Sam, running on ahead before I could throw a punch, "just weedy!"

"Weedy!" I cried, giving chase. "I'll show you weedy!" But Sam could run a hundred metres in twelve seconds, and with my little legs, I didn't stand a chance.

CONTEMPLATIONS ON BEING VERTICALLY CHALLENGED

All my friends
Take big size tens.
Me? Fours –
Narrow fitting.
(I still can't reach that old top drawer
Without a leg up off the floor.)
It is a cause of great concern
That all the blokes with birds to burn
Are always looking down their noses
At their lovely English Roses.
I want to grow,
I want to sprout,
I want to throw my Osh Kosh out.
I want a woman looking up;
To think of me as dog, not pup.
My life can only be despair
Until a girl at last does stare
All day upon my nostril hair!

(Johnny Casanova – from his short book, "Suicide's No Stranger – Fourteen Years of Hell and Misunderstanding")

4
DIABOLIC STEROIDS

I felt like victorious Hannibal returning home with his elephants as I cycled up the High Street a few minutes later. There was a swagger in my pedalling technique that impressed passers-by. I think it was quite obvious to them that I was now involved in a serious relationship, because old ladies smiled at me in an approving sort of a way, as if I was a respectable family man with responsibilities, and the lollipop lady let me cross the road on my own. That was brilliant. I hadn't felt this positive about myself since I came first on the quad link Road Race computer at the Trocadero. Bosie was obviously good for me, and the thought of going to The Freezer, my *first* nightclub, filled me full of delicious fear. What impressed me most though was that I was suddenly thinking like a grown-up, wrestling with abstract concepts, flirting with philosophy, that sort of thing. Like, for example, I suddenly understood why all rock songs were about love, because love really *is* a drug that consumes you, and when you're about eighteen or twenty you can't think about anything else. Nothing else matters. Not even eating. Bosie had unlocked a whole different side to my brain. It was freaky.

One thing still niggled, though. That little word, "weedy". I mean, I could see what Sam was driving at. Even though I'd matured into manhood on the inside, on the outside I was still only marginally stronger than the Queen Mother (actually she's probably got bigger biceps than me, what with lifting all those corgis all day and trying on hats), and if Bosie really did prefer big men, maybe I ought to beef myself up. Not out of vanity, you understand, it would just be a practical thing, to smooth the cracks in our relationship *before* they appeared. That's what adults do.

That's to say all adults except my parents, because they behave like children. When I got home, a police car was slewed across the carport with its doors open, and a couple of policeboys in blue uniforms were giving Sam's dad and my dad a dressing down. Apparently, they'd been chucking rubbish at each other over the fence. The grass was littered with it. Dad didn't like Mr Driver's plans for stone-cladding his house and Mr Driver didn't like

Dad. Dad thought Mr Driver was common and lowering the tone of the neighbourhood and Mr Driver thought it couldn't get much lower since Dad was there. Mr Driver had a Northern accent and Dad didn't like that either. I was going to walk straight past and pretend that Dad wasn't related, but Mum came tearing out of the house like a whirling dervish, with a snickering Sherene tucked underneath her skirts.

"Where've you been?" she shrieked.

"Swimming trials," I said.

"Didn't I tell you that Pongo needed a bath before he goes to the vet's?"

"That's not for another couple of days," I mumbled. "Anyway, you could do it tomorrow." Mum took a sharp breath.

"Oh, could I, Johnny? When exactly? In-between the school runs and washing your pants, or after I've spent three hours cooking supper and taken Nan to Batty Bingo?"

"I think you should hit him for being tho rude," said Sherene.

Mum ignored her. "It's *your* dog who's having a life and death fart-plugging operation! We can't send him on to the slab unhygienic!"

"Yeah, all right," I said. I figured if I gave in she might calm down. I was wrong.

"You're just like your father! Self, self, self! Look at him. Pathetic little man."

"I heard that!" bellowed Dad. The brutal tone of his voice stopped Mum dead in her tracks. Her mouth crumpled and she looked like she was going to cry. I'd never noticed before, but she had hundreds of little lines round her eyes. She looked worn out.

"Sorry," I said. "I should have thought."

"It's not you, pumpkin." She put her hand behind my neck and kissed the top of my head. "It's him. Never lifts a finger round the house. Spends all his time these days picking sad little fights with the neighbours."

"It's not sad, you big blouse! It's a principle," shouted Dad.

"It's a waste of money!" yelled Mum.

"Get back in your kitchen!" came Dad's reply. At which nastiness, one of the policeboys drew his truncheon and told the pair of them to "Put a sock in it!" He didn't half look stupid and ineffectual, though, trying to stop them. A bit like King Canute trying to turn back the sea.

But a couple of minutes later the policeboy did get Dad on his hands and knees clearing up the mess, while Mr Driver looked on smugly and Mrs Driver made some fresh Italian coffee for the policeboys. This was when everything went pear-shaped.

"Very nice," said the copper with the cuppa. "Delicious brew, Mrs D."

"That's our new cappuccino coffee maker,"

she preened. "So much nicer than instant." Dad bristled, stood up, ignored the policeboy's order to get back to work, stormed indoors and demanded to know where the Argos catalogue was. Mum was washing Pongo in the sink.

"What do you want it for now?" she said, squeezing Pongo's tummy hard to extract the suds from his fur. He yelped and blew a battalion of bubbles into the water. They burst through the soap on the surface and saturated the room with the stench of rotten eggs.

"A coffee maker," he revealed.

"But we drink instant," said Mum, looking puzzled.

"Precisely," growled Dad. "If you think I'm letting the Drivers serve better coffee to the constabulary than me, then you're very much mistaken."

"But it's a waste of money," Mum protested.

"That," said Dad, "depends on who earns the money in the first place." Mum went horribly quiet after that. It wasn't her fault that she didn't work, she had to look after Sherene and me, but Dad wanted to make her think it was. I wanted to ask Mum if she was all right, but she rushed up to her bedroom and slammed the door. Dad went after her shouting that he was only trying to improve the working conditions in her kitchen, and if she couldn't see that she was a stupid old moo. I was left to pull Pongo out of the sink before he drowned. Then I slipped down the shops to seek an instant cure for my weedy physique, in the hope that it might secure from Bosie both respect and a lifelong commitment to daily snogging.

ON BEING A MAN IN A CHILD'S
BODY

I see the world now
Through the eyes of a man,
But when I lift shopping
It don't look like I can.

(Johnny Casanova – what are the job opportunities for a stick insect?)

I ran down to Mr Patel's SHOP HERE PLEASE SHOP. Since the loosening up of the laws relating to the supply of prescription drugs to the public, Mr Patel had started a lucrative line in bankrupt stock from the local chemist. Stuff that was past its sell-by-date, that sort of thing. Dodgy but cheap. A new fluorescent sign in the window announced that Mr Patel's emporium now sold MORE DIFFERENT THINGS THAN HARRODS, AND BETTER VALUE TOO! Mr Patel considered the Trades Description Act to be obsolete in a modern society based on free trade and private enterprise.

"I need something to make me grow," I explained.

"Outwards or upwards?" asked Mr Patel.

"Bothwards," I replied.

"Then that is easy, Johnny Casanova. Take a leaf out of my tree. Be lonely all the time. If you don't kill yourself, you will be eating lots of chocolate biscuits and ice-cream for the comfort food. This will be putting on your weight by the tonne – absolutely guaranteed." I stared at Mr Patel's belly and although it looked distinguished on him, I didn't want it sticking out on me.

"On second thoughts, I just want to grow upwards."

"Ah, this will be for the ladies I am suspecting," said Mr Patel, wisely.

"How did you know?" I gasped.

"I too was shrimpish once," winked the old man. "I too know what it is like to be staring up at a beautiful lady's armpit all night. Of course now," he sighed, "of course now I would give my right arm for the pleasure." Mr Patel was definitely not his normal chirpy self. He seemed older, more tired, more weighed down by problems; less fun to be with.

"So you haven't got anything to make me grow?"

"I have a most trendsetting pair of very

short trousers that will make you *look* like you have grown," he offered.

"Versace?" I asked.

"No, polyester," he replied. I shook my head.

"How about something to bulk me out?"

"If it is muscles you are after, Johnny, then we are talking diabolic steroids," said Mr Patel.

"You don't sell them here, do you?"

"Sadly, I do not. They are most dangerous and are wicked on sperms."

"Then I wouldn't want them anyway," I said quickly. "I'm of an age, Mr Patel, when I need every sperm I can get. No point hunting with an empty gun, eh?" Mr Patel looked lost, not to say disinterested in my joke. "I'll just have to pump some iron instead," I added quickly.

"Iron tablets I do have."

"No, I meant weight-lifting."

"Oh."

"Do you have any dumb-bells?"

"Ah." Mr Patel looked mortified. "Why is one always just running out of stock just when one needs it most?"

Which is how I came to be working out in the garden with six tins of family assortment biscuits hanging off either end of a Vileda Supermop.

ON WORKING OUT

Girls adore big muscles more,
Tightened like a drum skin.
Hammer thighs elicit sighs,
While six-pack tums their hearts win.
(I know all this because I read
A body-building mag in bed.)
The fairer sex love bulging pecs,
They like their bodies oily.
So how come after working out
I still look like a doily?

(Johnny Casanova – still puny after pumping my own body weight in custard creams)

5
A BIT MOODY

The work out didn't work. I had two days to go before the gala and there wasn't a pumped-up pec. in sight. Not even a slight swelling. I had a good mind to write a letter of complaint to the managing director of Peak Frean Biscuits and tell him what I thought of his body-building tins. There was only one thing for it. If I was going to be in top physical shape to impress Bosie in the pool, I needed a professional hand on my tiller.

"Are you quite certain it's an emergency?" said the appointments' secretary on the other end of the phone. "Only the doctor is very busy today."

"I'm stunted," I said. "How much more seriously ill do I need to be?"

"So you keep saying, but it's not an illness we can treat."

"I can't reach the cereals on the top of the fridge," I said.

"Then eat toast," came the acid retort.

"And it could be about to seriously affect my love life."

"I'm sorry, but we're not agony aunts," said the secretary.

"But I get dizzy spells," I added quickly, "and restricted vision."

"That'll be because you're short."

"No, that's because of the blinding headaches from the steel plate in my skull. Oh go on," I begged. "She must see me now. I'm telling the truth, honest." The secretary took a breath, but I jumped in before she could tell me for the millionth time that the emergency clinic was for emergencies only. "I'll be down in ten minutes," I said. "No, make that fifteen. Having extra spindly legs means I can't walk as fast as normal people."

I was sitting on my own in the surgery for five minutes before the doctor rushed in and banged my notes down on the desk. She had long thin fingers like pick-a-sticks, useful for rummaging around in people's intestines, I thought, and brown hair with a bizarre grey streak down the centre of her fringe.

"Sorry I'm late," she said briskly. "I've been choking some haemorrhoids. Now, what's wrong with you?"

"I've stopped growing," I said.

"Did you ever start?" came the oh-so-witty response. How would she like it if I told her she looked like a badger? "This is the fourth time I've seen you this month," she said, studying my notes.

"I've got problems," I said.

"You're not the only one," she muttered, fixing me with an accusing stare. "How old are you, Johnny?"

"Fourteen."

"And you don't think that this succession of phantom illnesses might have something to do with the onset of puberty?" There was that word. When it was used in class we giggled, because it sounded like pubic. I bit my lip and stared at my knees. "To date, you have come to me suffering from a squeaky voice, black hairs in your armpits and pubic region—" A snort squidged through my lips before I could stifle it. "Have I said something to amuse you?" she asked coldly before reeling off the rest of my medical history. "A bottomless hole in your stomach, a disliking of your face, growing pains in your knees and ankles, a loathing of your parents, an obsession with mirrors, and most significant of all, a need to lie down in a pit of a bedroom while the rest of your family bonds round the telly downstairs." She closed my notes. "And you don't think there's a pattern here?"

"Not really," I said. "If it was ... that thing you said—"

"Puberty," she said loudly, putting my maturity to the test.

"Yeah, that thing, I should be filling out in the chest region, shouldn't I? And I'm not."

"That's because you're not a girl," said the doctor, "in case you hadn't noticed." I sighed in the face of such anatomical wit. To tell the truth, I think all medical students should be strangled at birth to prevent them from inflicting their puerile humour on the rest of us.

"I meant *muscular* development of the chest!" I said.

"People grow differently," she explained. "Let's check you out. Stand up."

"The problem is—" I said.

"Loosen your belt."

"...that I'm diving in a gala tomorrow—"

"Undo your button."

"...and I've got to impress Bosie—"

"Drop your jeans."

"And then I'm going to The Freezer where I really want to dance with her, but what if I haven't got the strength to hold on to her when she leaps up and locks her legs round my neck?"

"And cough."

"Blimey! What the hell are you doing?" The doctor had just shoved her hand down the front of my underpants and grabbed my todger! No kiss, nothing! "Your hands are freezing!" I squealed.

"You're fine," she said. "You can pull your trousers back up again now." That was easier said than done. After the initial shock, the examination had proved to be something of a turn on and my trousers were rather tight. I turned away and ever so carefully zipped up my flies. When I turned back my cheeks were piping hot and the doctor was washing her hands at the sink. I smiled at her in case it hadn't been an examination at all, but a blatant pass from a frustrated older woman (and I wasn't missing out on a bit of hands-on sex education if it was going begging) but she carried on rinsing without a trace of tenderness.

"Is that it?" I asked, killing the smile.

"Yes," she said. "It's puberty all right. You'll find yourself experiencing uncontrollable mood swings and also feelings of low self-esteem. It's perfectly normal."

I laughed out loud. "Me? Mood swings! Never! I'm at the peak of my happiness. I'm hot to trot!"

"Really?" said the doctor, without much enthusiasm.

"So when can I expect to get manly?"

"Soon," she sighed. "Probably next Tuesday. And if it takes a little longer, I shouldn't worry. You've got a nice body, Johnny. Be happy with it." She pressed the intercom.

"Next patient. And please don't come back unless it's something really serious."

Doctors! Who needs them? What was the point of telling me I might be manly next Tuesday when the gala was on Friday? Hadn't she listened to a word I was saying? And what was all that claptrap about mood swings? I wasn't moody. I was in love. Which was why I was getting so het up about Bosie seeing me podge-naked. I didn't want my body to upset her. Call herself a doctor! The only thing she said that made any sense was telling me I had a nice body. The memory of which gave me goose-bumps down my arms and a warm sort of glow where my heart was. There's nothing quite like a compliment to restore one's ego, is there? And once restored, I started thinking more clearly. Bosie had already seen my body. If she was going to find my body repulsive she'd have said something at the trials, wouldn't she? Of course she would. So much for feelings of low self-esteem! In one fell swoop I had disproved each and every one of this backstreet quack's theories, which only goes to show that doctors are about as much use as a deaf dog at a sheep trial.

By the time I got home, the weedy issue was history and I'd already mentally leap-frogged back into Bosie's bed. Dad was in the kitchen unpacking the cappuccino coffee maker that he'd sneakily bought at Argos while Mum was down the supermarket. Pongo, still waiting for his operation, was slumped across the floor in a pool of his own froth, Sherene was measuring breast implants in her *Baywatch Annual* and Nan was knitting quietly in the corner.

"Got to keep our boys warm," she muttered, pulling another length of wool off the khaki ball on her knee.

"What's she talking about?" I whispered.

"Humour her," said Dad. "She's knitting scarves for soldiers. Thinks she's helping the war effort."

"What war?" I said.

"World War Two."

"Mr Churchill only wears cashmere," said Nan.

"Not any more," I told her. "He's dead."

"Dead!" cried the old woman, dropping her needles. "But without Mr Churchill we'll never beat the Bosch!" Dad was looking daggers at me, like I was some sort of German spy or something, when Mum staggered through the back door, weighed down by the weekly shop. A bag of sprouts rolled across the kitchen table and bounced off the floor when she saw what he'd bought.

"What?" he protested innocently. "What have I done now?" Like he didn't know exactly what.

"What's that?" she hissed.

"It's your new cappuccino machine," he

replied cheerfully. You could tell he was lying by the way he scratched the back of his neck.

"But I don't want it," said Mum. "I drink instant, remember?"

"It's a gift," said Dad, scratching harder.

"It's a waste of money," snapped Mum. "You swan out like the Duke of bloomin' Westminster and buy yourself coffee makers, but I can't spend a penny on myself. Is that the way it is?"

"You're beautiful as you are, babe." If Dad scratched much more he'd be through to the bone.

"I'm past my sell-by-date," said Mum.

"Look," Dad said, rising from the table and plugging the machine in, "let me make you a cappuccino. You'll feel better for it."

"No," replied Mum sharply, "let me make you one, Terry."

"That's it. That's the spirit," encouraged Dad. "I knew you'd like the machine when you got used to it. I'll be in the garden when it's ready." Mum flashed him a savage smile as he left.

"He'th building a catapult with one of your brath to fire thithtleth and weedth into Mr Driver'th garden," announced Sherene, as Mum fizzed with fury, snatched a mug off the draining board and filled it with half-brewed coffee from the machine. "He didn't want you to know, becauthe you'd be angry, but I thaw him." Mum wasn't listening. She was maniacally scraping Pongo's flobber off the floor with her fingers and spreading it over the surface of the coffee so it looked like a frothy white head.

"Yoo-hoo, darling," she called. "Your delicious cappuccino's ready!" And she carried it out on a silver tray with all the cool-headedness of a master poisoner.

ADOLESCENT ADULTS

If puberty means moody rages
Mum and Dad are still teenagers.

(Johnny Casanova – more perception
than your average pair of parents)

While Mum and Dad played Borgias in the garden and Sherene shoved tights up one of Mum's bikinis to make herself look voluptuous like Pamela Anderson, I skipped upstairs for an unexpurgated fantasy about me and Bosie. We were in The Freezer. She was running across the dance floor towards me in her zebra-print microskirt, arms outstretched, eyes alive with longing, lips like stoned cherries. She was calling out my name and brushing off all the other poor saps who were making a grab for her. Keanu Reeves, Johnny Depp, Brad Pitt, all fell by the wayside in her desperate desire to reach me. She threw her arms around my neck, ran her fingers through the knots in my hair, tickled her nose 'twixt my ear and cheek, and then, just as our quivering lips strained to connect, she said, "You're the prat who's never heard of Elastic Strawberry, aren't you?"

The fantasy exploded in a mushroom cloud of self-loathing. I mean, what sort of sick mind did I have to invent a killer question like that just before a French kiss? I knew I didn't know who Elastic Strawberry were, so why did I put the words in her mouth? Because I was punishing myself for being a rock 'n' roll virgin, I guess; for not knowing whether Elastic Strawberry were heavy metal, rap, techno, lesbian aggressive, glam, grunge, house, punk, jungle, hardcore, scuzz, flim-flam, fuzz or gospel.

This was one of those low self-esteem trips that the doctor had warned me about. Somewhere inside my warped head there was a devil planting seeds of self-doubt in the gardens of my mind. I started to panic, but the more I panicked the more the weeds of low self-esteem grew. I wasn't just ignorant about music, I was ignorant about LIFE! I had so much to learn if I was to become an interesting boyfriend, and no time to do it in. It was like there was a vast finger pointing out of the sky and a voice booming, "It's you!" Only I hadn't won the lottery or anything useful like that, I was being singled out as the most stupid person on the planet. I didn't know anything about anything. I was a Grade A thicko and Bosie would see straight through me. One passing comment about Northern Ireland or Tony Blair's toothpaste and I'd be dead in the water. What was I going to talk to her about? Dog medicine? I could hardly woo Bosie with the nitty gritty of Pongo's anal scrapings. Even Ginger was more interesting than me. At the very least he could talk about judo and having naturally red hair, but everything I knew I'd learned off the back of a Cornflake packet. Suddenly I wished I'd paid attention in class instead of constantly dropping my pencil case to squint up the teacher's skirt. I felt hopelessly inadequate. I'd never worn cufflinks, or hailed a cab, or drunk alcohol, or held a baby, or been to Paris, or put a bet on a horse, or even read Jane Austen! Why wasn't I interesting? Why didn't I know what I liked? Why was I putting myself through this date? Just to make a titanic tit of myself, that's why!

MOODY ME

Hormonally I'm all mixed up,
My moods are quite unstable,
Emotionally I'm like a soup –
A murky veg-e-table.
Had Darwin (Charles) still been alive

And studied me with science,
I think I'd now be classified
A Kitchen Food Appliance.
Observing how my feelings churn,
He'd powwow with professors,
To catalogue my parents as
A pair of Food Processors.

(Johnny Casanova – pouring turmoil
on troubled waters)

Maybe the doctor was right. Maybe I *was* a victim of the puberty plague. Maybe this was a mood swing. I mean, half an hour ago I'd been sitting in a deckchair on Cloud Nine, sipping celestial cocktails. Now, I'd dug myself into a black hole of insecurity and I didn't know why. If I carried on at this rate, they'd be fishing me out of the Thames in six months. I had to get a grip of my hormones. I mean it wasn't as if Bosie had phoned me to tell me it was over. It wasn't as if she'd phoned and told me to stay away from her at the gala tomorrow, because the sight of me might put her off her stroke!

I froze right there!

The gala! I started to choke. It felt like I had a small furry mammal wedged in my throat. My black mood skidded on black ice and somersaulted on to the hard shoulder of hysteria. Gala! Trunks! I still hadn't bought a pair of green trunks! I DIDN'T HAVE ANY GREEN TRUNKS! If I didn't have any green trunks, Miss Percival wouldn't let me compete. If I didn't compete, then I wouldn't impress Bosie. If I didn't impress Bosie, she'd cancel The Freezer. If she cancelled The Freezer, my life would be at an end! Was a strip of green lycra what now stood between me and lifelong happiness? I think I must have screamed.

"Are you all right?" whispered a voice through the bannisters. It was Nan crawling up the stairs on her knees. "I heard you wail."

"For the sake of a pair of green trunks," I whimpered, "I've lost the girl I love!"

"Nonsense," said Nan. "That's defeatist talk that is. Where would Mr Churchill be today if he'd talked like that?"

"Mr Churchill didn't need green trunks," I said.

"You leave it to me," winked Nan. "Did nobody ever tell you I've got magic fingers?" Then she climbed the ladder to her loft and disappeared up her bolt hole.

Reassured that Nan was now sorting the trunks trauma, I flopped gratefully into bed. The warm duvet soothed my moody mind and chilled out the tension in my body. I gazed romantically out of the window at the moon and the stars and shivered with delicious synchronicity. I imagined Bosie lying in crisp, cool sheets gazing at the same sparkling cluster. For centuries lovers had done this – come together spiritually via the Milky Way – and it was fitting that I should join their club. One star was brighter than all the rest. It sparkled like an iron-flecked pebble catching the sun's rays underwater. In the name of love, it was crying out to be christened. I called it Johnny Casanova and its smaller, dimmer cousin, Bosie. Our love was truly made in Heaven. This was what I was thinking when I heard a noise outside. It started with a twang and ended with a cry of pain that put me in mind of a piglet being castrated with a pair of electrical pliers.

It was only in the morning that I discovered it was Dad.

THE SIMPLE ART OF DIVING AT A
GALA IN FRONT OF BOSIE

Self-belief is all I need,
Who says my dive's appalling?
Yes, confidence will be the seed;
A dive is only falling.
It can't be hard to twist and turn,
Or touch my toes for Bosie,
A triple pike's a cinch to learn,
A jackknife easy-posy.
I spit on speed, I laugh at pain,
Let me split my skull again!
Diving into swimming pools

Is something you can teach to fools.
Tomorrow, then, when up I climb,
Atop that diving-tower,
When time's immortal hands do point
Towards the appointed hour,
The trembling crowd will see no fear,
Nor yellow-bellied scream will hear,
For I will shock the populace
By leaping like a frog.
I'll dive right into B's embrace,
The crowd will be agog!

(Johnny Casanova – this is one
learner diver who intends to pass the
test)

6
IN AT THE DEEP END

Nan came through like a trooper. At breakfast the next morning, she appeared with bags under her eyes.

"I sat up all night," she said, "but I did it." Then she produced a pair of knitted trunks from behind her back. "I only had khaki wool," she explained, "for the troops, but it's still green."

"Thanks," I said, taking possession of the largest pair of swimming trunks known to man.

"Lucky I found an old piece of knicker elastic in my sewing box or they'd keep falling down!"

Lucky, she said. Lucky! These trunks were four times the size of Timothy Winchester's. Nan's extra large needles had produced stitches that were two centimetres across, that's thicker than a garden worm, giving the trunks the appearance and texture of medieval chain mail, although God help any knight who'd worn these into combat – steel armour would've felt like a lightweight safari suit by comparison. She said she'd followed an old pattern for lederhosen, but hadn't bothered with the braces in case I thought they looked stupid.

"No danger of that," I said tersely. I mean, who'd be laughing at braces when the legs of the costume were flying at half-mast just above my ankles. Without wishing to offend Nan, they weren't swimming trunks, they were swimming trousers, but there was certainly no denying they were green.

"You'll be well camouflaged in those," she said proudly, which was a bonus, I must say. Who else in the swimming squad could dive off the Bridge on the River Kwai and not get shot by the Japs? What was she thinking? The waist was drawn in extra tight by several bands of knicker elastic and was tinier than a Polo mint, and there was a little hole cut in the front, which I could only presume was there for reasons of hygiene. "That's for spending a penny," beamed Nan. I was right.

"They're ... er—" I couldn't find a word to describe them— "unbelievable," I choked. "And you made them just for me?"

"So you could go out and impress that girl!" she winked.

"Well, they're certainly going to make an impression," I said. Although probably not the one I was hoping for. "You shouldn't have." Nan blushed. "No, really," I added, "I mean it, you shouldn't have." Fortunately Dad backed into the kitchen at that precise moment, which saved me having to strangle Nan for cocking up my big day before it had even begun. He was dragging a pig's head through the door and leaving a streak of brown blood across the lino. Sherene screamed and leapt up from the table disturbing the bluebottles feeding inside the carcass. They swarmed in panic towards the closed window and splatted like kamikaze pilots against the glass.

"I think I'm going to thpew!" retched Sherene. "What'th that?"

"Payback!" growled Dad menacingly, his eyebrows locked in black rage. It was only then that I noticed he was wearing flip-flops and his toes were all bandaged.

"Is that what that piglet noise was last night?" I asked, pointing to his swollen feet.

"That Northern monster buried mousetraps in our flowerbed, Johnny. Can you believe it? It was like walking on a minefield!" It wasn't really the moment to point out that Dad was just as much to blame for catapulting weeds into Mr Driver's garden with Mum's bra. "I nicked this pig's head out the dustbin at the

Rotary Club," he went on. "The Boy Scouts had a hog roast last weekend." He laughed grotesquely, like a bad pantomime villain, as he and the pig slid out of the back door and disappeared round the side of the house. I think Dad was ever so slightly losing it. Just then, Mum walked briskly into the kitchen, wobbled slightly and popped two Alka-Seltzer into a glass of water.

"Anyone notice anything different about me this morning?" she trilled.

"Apart from your purple hair, you mean?" I said.

"That's it," she beamed. "Do you like it? I did it myself, just now."

"You look like a blackberry," said Sherene. "Dad'th going to be furiouth."

"That, pumpkin, is the idea," she grinned, only it wasn't a soft smile, it was hard like thin glass. "Anyone seen the old git yet?"

"He'th outthide with a yucky pig," said Sherene. But he wasn't, because even as Sherene spoke, Dad came crashing through the back door, panting like a dog who's been chasing squirrels.

"You'll never believe what Driver's done now!" he fumed. "He's just taken delivery of a new car!"

"Do you like my hair, dear?" asked Mum.

"He's done it to shame us. Well that's it, anything he can do, I can do better!"

"And my hair?"

"I'm taking the car and selling it," said Dad, snatching up the car keys and heading outdoors again.

"But what about my hair?"

"Very nice," he called over his shoulder.

"No, it's NOT very nice. It's disgusting!" screamed Mum. "Because I can't afford to go to the hairdresser's to have it done properly, because you've spent all our money playing Cowboys and Indians with the little boy next door!"

"New cars don't come cheap, Babs."

Mum shot out of the door after him, while Sherene and I went to the window to eavesdrop. "Then don't buy one, Tel!"

"Got to have a new car, poppet."

"But I need to take Pongo to the vet's."

"Use the bus!" shouted Dad, and with that he jumped in the old Allegro, reversed into the road with a screech, knocked the number plate off on the kerb and smoked tyre like a macho cop in "The Sweeney".

When I left for school, minutes later, I was heavy of heart and even heavier of rucksack (thanks to Nan's trunks). I wheeled my bike down the path and sighed publicly as I prepared to greet the naffest day of my life.

"Problem?" asked Sam, who was standing by the fence, waiting for a lift to school.

"Bosie's going to hate me when she sees my trunks," I said, sounding like the world had just ended, "they look like woolly long johns. Mum and Dad are on the verge of a divorce, Nan thinks Hitler's already landed and nobody's told her, and Ginger, the greedy git, has got himself a harem. Apart from that..." I kicked a pebble into the gutter. "How are you?"

"Fine," said Sam. "I've lost a pencil sharpener, my shoelaces won't stay done up, and my socks itch, but apart from that ... it's a beautiful day for a suicide."

I had to smile. "Sorry. It's this gala. It's making me nervous. My future happiness is at stake."

"All you've got to do is fall into water," said Sam. "What can go wrong?"

"Bosie," I said. "What if she doesn't like the way I fall?"

"You can only do your best," said Sam, as Mr Driver emerged through the front door with a face as cocky as a bloke who'd just sold penguin pie to the Eskimos. He was still glorying in his mousetrap victory over Dad. He told Sam to hop into the new car and opened the driver's door to get in himself, when suddenly he stopped short and let out a gutteral explosion which sounded like a Spaceball puncturing on sharp rocks. When his face reappeared over the roof of the car it was as black as old boot leather. Dad had skewered the pig's head on a stake and propped it up in front of the steering wheel so it looked like it was driving. There was a note pinned to one of its ears, which said, *Road Hog!* Mr Driver was having a convulsion. He could hardly breathe as he dragged the pork surprise out of his precious car.

"This is war!" he snarled, as he shoved Sam into the car. Then he slid across the bloody seat, gunned the gas and shot off up the street in a cloud of carbon monoxide.

At school, Miss Percival said she had some really good news. She'd arranged for the entire school to miss afternoon lessons so they could support the swimming squad. I could have killed her. The prospect of a thousand-strong crowd at the gala turned my guts inside out and I considered chucking myself under one of the coaches that turned up to take us to the baths, but Nan's three-tonne trunks weighted me to the pavement and I couldn't move, let alone jump.

I was sitting with Ginger halfway up the coach, while Bosie was larking about at the back with Sharon and Darren. Sharon had cut her hair short, dyed the stubble jet black and had got a new stud through her nose.

"I did it for Darren," I heard her tell Bosie. "He likes a pierced body, does Darren."

"I do," confirmed her face-dead dork of a boyfriend, "and Sharon's going to be my perfect woman."

"That's why I'm having my belly-button done next week," she giggled. "Darren's coming with me."

"To get my tongue pierced," he said. "I've always wanted a metal tongue, but never dared. Sharon's given me the strength. She's so alive. That's why we connect. We're wild childs."

Please, I thought, do us all a favour and have your tongue stapled to the roof of your mouth. What a tragic pair of fashion victims these two were. Where was their self-respect? Couldn't they just be themselves for once, instead of always trying to be what the other wanted? When I asked Ginger if he agreed with my damning assessment of Sharon and Darren, he muttered something about the pot calling the kettle black and asked me what I thought I was doing by taking up diving to impress Bosie.

"What do you mean?" I said. "I love her." But Ginger wouldn't be drawn further. He was reading his judo manual, swotting up for his First Mon, and didn't want me bugging him. So I turned round to watch Bosie in the hope that she might be watching me, but she wasn't. After about twenty minutes, by which time my neck had gone into spasm, she finally glanced in my direction and smiled briefly across the aisle. Only it wasn't a simmering smile full of lusty promise, it was a casual one, the sort you'd give to a passing acquaintance when you met them in Safeway with their mum. I was gutted. I snatched Ginger's manual out of his hands and sat on it.

"I need to talk," I said. "What am I doing wrong with Bosie?"

"I don't think you're doing anything wrong," he said.

"But she's not lusting for me."

"You've only just met her," he sighed. "You're expecting too much too soon."

"But she's my ideal woman," I explained.

"Last week your ideal woman was that leggy blonde you saw sneezing outside the chemist, remember?"

"But I was much younger then," I said defensively.

"You told me you didn't care what a woman looked like so long as she had legs up to her armpits," he added brutally.

"Yeah, well I'm fourteen now," I snapped back. "I've matured. I still love legs, but I also love arms and heads now too, OK?" Which fit of pique rather put the kibosh on any further discussion. Ginger wrenched his manual out from under my knees and I wallowed in a mire of self-doubt. My dive was going to have to be pretty spectacular to capture Bosie's tepid heart.

WORRY

Worry is a curry,
'Cause it makes your brain cells boil!

(Johnny Casanova – worried that the lines don't rhyme)

I entered the changing room in a tortured mental state. It got worse when I realized that all of the other boys (hundreds of them from about twenty different schools) were wearing body-hugging Speedo trunks with padded posing pouches. Nan's mega-knit trouser-trunks promised all the sexiness of a potato sack. If a teacher hadn't shut the door behind me and told us to hurry up, I think I'd've hidden in a locker and not come out for anybody, not even Bosie. As it was I was trapped. I found myself a cubicle with a door and pulled it shut. I must have been right under the spectator's gallery, because the noise from the poolside was phenomenal. The whole wall was buzzing with it. There must have been a thousand people out there waiting to laugh at my trunks. I took a deep breath and dropped my strides. The nightmare had begun!

I waited till the changing room was empty before coming out. The waistband sawed me in half as I walked. Force of habit made me check my hair in the mirror. It was kicking, which was more than could be said for my legs. From the waist down I looked like a khaki llama.

"Johnny Worms to poolside," demanded the loudspeaker on the ceiling by the showers.

I felt sick. The wiry wool chafed the soft skin between my legs as I took the longest, loneliest walk of my life, out through the tunnel and into the glare of the lion's den. My appearance was greeted by stunned silence. Bosie was staring nervously at the scoreboard, and twanging the elasticated leg holes of her costume. I knew it. I was too shameful to look at. God, was I a dork!

Then a child in the crowd shouted, "Why's that boy wearing a lawn?" and the mob burst out laughing. They mocked my trunks from all sides with wild hoots of derision and stamping of hysterical feet.

"Good heavens!" gasped the man on the tannoy, stifling a snort, then coughing to regain his composure. "You must be Johnny Worms." Now they all knew my name! I bowed my head. "Well, now that you're here, we can start. Take a seat." The man on the tannoy paused for a moment. "You *can* sit down in those trunks, I take it?" More humiliating guffaws from the crowd. I fixed the cause of my abasement with a long, cold stare, which left him in no doubt that if he had a problem with my trunks, it was but a piffle compared to mine.

The High Dive was, as you'd expect, the last event in the gala, which meant I had to sit there, suffering the crowd's relentless stare for three and a half hours. By the time they called my name, our school was jointly in the lead with a bunch of toffee-nosed gits from the country. Bosie had walked past me several times during the competition without speaking, but now she approached me as my team captain.

I was hoping for soothing words of encouragement. Instead I got this, "Me and the rest of the team don't care that you look like a tit, we just want you to win. OK?" It was just the sort of pep talk I didn't need.

"Divers in the pool, please," said the man on the tannoy. I struggled to my feet and jumped in without a thought for what was going to happen next. You know how a single sponge can soak up a troughful of water? Well, woollen trunks are fifty times more absorbent. Over the next few seconds, they not only sucked up water faster than a troop of thirsty elephants, but they grew as well. I had to be helped out of the pool. The trunks were so long that they dragged along the tiles and so heavy that my knees buckled twice on the way round to the diving-tower.

It took me fifteen minutes to climb forty-three steps. By the time I reached the platform,

I was sweating profusely and utterly exhausted. I had lost about seven kilograms in weight and my head was spinning from massive dehydration. I refocused my eyes, staggered towards the edge of the board and looked down. It was terrifying, like standing on the top of Niagara Falls. I felt giddy and would have tumbled forward had I not been so firmly rooted to the platform by half a mile of sodden knitwear. I closed my eyes and raised my arms above my head. This was it! I had to put the embarrassment of my bathing bags behind me if I was to perform to Bosie's satisfaction and win her heart. I took a deep breath and composed myself, running through the complexities of the dive in my mind. Then I flew up into the air, one forward roll, then a second, a twist, a turn and then another. My trunks were just too heavy. With a twang that ricocheted off the glass roof, the knicker elastic snapped, and the trunks shot upwards off my waist like a released parachute and followed me down into the water. My entry was perfect, but I had no clothes on.

Getting out of the bath is hard enough, if you've got a mum like mine who sneakily tries to check the development of your love muscle, but climbing out of a swimming pool with two thousand gawping eyes peering at your naked nadgers takes the biscuit. It was worse than reading the lesson at assembly and discovering halfway through that you've got a giant, green gilbert hanging out of your nose like a grass snake. I stood upright in the water and kicked my way to the edge, cleverly using the ripples to obscure my undercarriage, but heaving myself out of the pool required both hands, and nothing was left to the crowd's imagination when, like King Neptune, I sprang from the depths, as pink as a prawn, only not quite so big. Maintaining my dignity, I placed a hand front and rear and side-shuffled into the changing room, with the sound of cheers and laughter ringing in my ears.

As I shivered in that cold cubicle I knew for certain that Bosie was lost to me for ever. I had to cast her from my mind and concentrate on starting my life over, preferably in Australia with a new name.

"Go away," I groaned, as someone knocked on the door.

"Are you decent in there?" asked the voice outside.

"Does it matter?" I replied. "The whole world's seen what I've got." The door flew open. It was Bosie.

"And very nice it was too," she smiled, wickedly. "You were magnificent." I was confused. Did she mean my diving or my p...? "We won!" she shrieked. She meant my diving.

"How?"

"You scored six perfect marks!"

"Does that mean I can still come to The Freezer tomorrow?" I asked.

"Come outside and meet my parents," she said, which I took to mean yes.

I was greeted like a champion when Bosie escorted me into the foyer. Boys' hands ruffled my hair and girls' lips brushed my cheeks as we pushed our way through the excited throng to the Coke machine.

"Mummy and Daddy, this is Johnny," said Bosie shoving me forward to shake their hands.

"Unusual style," said her grey-haired father, stiffly. His dark blue suit had creases down the sleeves.

"I'm surprised you can dive with all that hair," trilled Bosie's mother, who was wearing a string of pearls the size of golf balls. Bosie laughed politely at her mother's joke.

"Yes," said her father, adjusting his half-moon glasses and peering down his nose at my dripping hair. He sucked his teeth disapprovingly. "Come along, dear, we'd best be going." But before they could leave their path was blocked by a screeching klaxon with big purple hair.

"Cooeee! Pumpkin!" It was Mum. "Have we missed your display?"

"Yes," I said. I didn't tell her *what* I'd displayed.

"Sorry I'm late," she prattled, "but I had to pick up Pongo from the vet's."

"Our dog," I explained.

"He's had a little operation to stop up his colon," she added, just to complete the pretty picture for Mr and Mrs Cricket.

"Mum!" I hissed.

"Am I embarrassing you, Johnny?" What could I say?

"Of course not," I lied.

"Good," she said, "because I need your help in the car-park. I've just had a little accident in your dad's new car. It's all the garage's fault for putting first gear so close to reverse." My stomach clenched like a knotted elastic band. She was more embarrassing than a fart in a lift. Bosie's mother and father had cowered at the loud intrusion. "Well, come on, pumpkin. Don't dawdle. I need your muscles to untangle the metal bits before the owners of the other car come back."

Unfortunately, the owners of the other car were Mr and Mrs Cricket, and when they saw the state of their Mercedes Estate, Mrs Cricket burst into tears. Mr Cricket was more reserved. His face turned as purple as Mum's hair and his left eye started twitching. Mum whinnied nervously like a horse and I caught sight of Bosie with her head in her hands. Why is there never a hole in the ground when you need one?

PLEASE, GOD, LET THIS STOP

When I'm older,
I'll invent
A hole
The size of
Eastern Kent.
I'll make it
So it folds
Up small,
To fit inside
A matchbox.
Then, whenever
Kith and kin
Give me
Cause for
Blushing skin,
(By being so embarrassing),
I'll do the things as following:
Unlock the box,
Unroll the hole,
Farewell the hell,
And jump right in!

(Johnny Casanova – wishing I'd been born an orphan)

My embarrassment did not end at the sight of Mr and Mrs Cricket's mangled bumper, nor at Mum's confusion over remembering the name of her insurance company, which caused her to sweat like a horse and made the purple dye run down her forehead and neck, nor even at the sight of Pongo in the back of the car with a blue bucket over his head. No, my embarrassment reached its peak when I saw Dad's new car – it was a Lada. A two-stroke shoebox on wheels! Didn't Dad realize that being seen in a Lada was even more seriously uncool than wearing jeans from Marks & Spencers? Only flatheads drove Ladas. Only total brain-deads bought them, which just about summed up my dad – chairman of the crappy car-coat brigade! There was only one way to handle this. I turned my back on the lot of them and walked home.

Behind me I could hear my mum crunch the gearbox and grind the complaining car into first gear. With the engine screaming, I heard the two bumpers tear apart and the Lada's front bumper clatter to the road like an aluminium pipe-cleaner. Then I heard Dad's love of his life (that's the Lada, not Mum) shoot out of the car-park towards me. Mum stopped the car in the middle of the road and threw open the passenger door.

"Go away," I said. "I don't know you."

"Get in!" she bellowed. The tendons in her neck stood out so far that her head looked like the Eiffel Tower. I squeezed in next to the twisted bumper.

"Dad's going to be pleased," I said, with as

much sarcasm as I could muster.

"Just shut up!" she snapped. Her eyes were wide and staring like a kitten's. I thought they were going to pop. Then I realized she was crying.

"Bosie's never going to speak to me again," I muttered sorrowfully. "Thanks to you."

Neither of us spoke again for several minutes. Then Mum said, "Bums!" and nobody spoke for a few minutes more.

Mum was wittery-jittery by the time we got home. She was convinced that Dad would have a heart attack when he saw what she'd done to the car. (Chance'd be a fine thing!) She switched off the engine as we turned into our road.

"Go and see where he is," she whispered, although why she was whispering when we were inside a sealed car, five hundred metres from our front door, God alone knows!

Dad was busy in the back garden building a rocket launcher out of several lengths of plastic piping and a bicycle pump. Next to him, on a tray, he had chunks of slaughtered mad cow sweating in the sunshine, ready to use as ammunition. In the carport he'd lashed Sherene's trampoline to two heavy poles, which he'd sunk into the flowerbed, facing Mr Driver's front door.

"What's that for?" I asked.

"In case he retaliates after I've bombarded

him," twitched Dad. "It's a movable shield, Johnny, to bounce his missiles back when he shoots at our new car. Can't have him wrecking the paintwork with vinegar bombs." I left Dad absorbed in his make-believe weapons of war and signalled to Mum that the coast was clear for her to drive in. She edged the Lada up to the front wall of the house until the headlamps were three inches away from the brickwork. Then I wedged the bumper between the house and the car so that it looked like it was attached. We were just in time. Dad hurried over as Mum stepped out, and ran his hands over the Lada's bodywork.

"Isn't she a beauty?" he trembled excitedly. "Ooh, she's still warm under the bonnet! How did she handle, love? Like a dream, I bet." Yeah, I thought, a bad one. Mum just smiled weakly and tried to change the subject by remarking how pretty she thought the rocket launcher looked, but Dad only had eyes for his new lump of scrap metal. "It'll look lovely after I've polished it up," he said. "Two years without holidays and we'll have paid for it."

"How much?" whimpered Mum.

"Only £4,500," said Dad proudly. "A real bargain."

"Only?!" I spluttered. Mum just closed her eyes.

"I knew you'd be impressed."

"Doeth the engine work?" asked Sherene,

who had been helping a poot-free Pongo out of the car when the door handle had come off in her hand. "Or hath the elathtic band broken?"

It had been a long day, but the night was to prove even longer. My need to kiss Bosie was physical. When I thought about her lips my stomach hurt like I had food poisoning, but when I drifted towards sleep and fantasized about touching their warm mushiness, I kept seeing Mum's face peering over Bosie's shoulder, saying, "And another thing, pumpkin. I've decided to stand here for ever, just to make sure you never ever, ever get sexy together, all right." She'd made a right dork of herself this afternoon. Bosie probably wouldn't even look at me tomorrow at The Freezer and if she did it would only be with contempt. Misery made a cold bedfellow indeed and no amount of shower catalogue browsing could change that.

At about ten thirty the phone rang. I was surprised when Mum screeched that it was for me. I slid out of bed in a daze and answered it on the landing.

"Hello," I mumbled.

"Hi," said Bosie. "Just wanted to say goodnight." Bosie! I was standing talking to Bosie without any clothes on. "You weren't in bed were you?"

"No way," I said casually, and I modestly

covered up in case she could see me. "I never go to bed before midnight. How's the car?"

"The insurance are paying," she said. "I don't see what all the fuss was about—"

"Sorry about my mad mum," I butted in.

"She was funny," said Bosie.

"But you had your head in your hands."

"I didn't want my parents to see me laughing. You're just like her, you know."

"Am I?"

"Funny, I mean. So, are you coming to The Freezer?" I was in such a state of shock that my voice deserted me. I answered with a pervy grunt.

"See you there, then. Night." Then the phone went dead, and I stood there, in the buff, for at least ten minutes before I put the receiver down.

That night, I had a weird dream, which went like this:

I'm standing at the fridge with a large piece of cheese, and I'm waving it under Mum and Dad's noses and luring them out into the shed with the smell of it. And they're following, like two blind mice, and I open the door to the shed and chuck the cheese in. And when they're inside I slam the door and lock it with three padlocks and wait for the traps to spring, which they do with a whistling thunk, like a huge dart embedding itself in a totem pole.

And when I open the door I'm an orphan and Mum and Dad are as dead as spiked dormice. I must be the first murderer in the history of murderers to have successfully used a mouse-trap as a fatal weapon. Then I go back indoors, pack a bag for Sherene and send her off to boarding school with a £20 note and strict instructions never to contact me again.

Then I go to the bank, collect my inheritance and board a plane at Heathrow. Only when I get to the top of the boarding steps, I'm standing on a diving-board with no clothes on and Bosie's floating on a red-lipped lilo in the heart-shaped pool beneath me, making a telephone call. And suddenly there's a buzzing in my trunks, which is weird, because I was naked last time I looked. So I answer the phone and Bosie purrs on the other end like a pussy cat and tells me to "Come on in, the water's lovely." So I do. I take the plunge and dive in to get her, but when I break the surface, I'm not in a pool any more. I'm on a muscle beach in Barbados, where pecs are power and Bosie brings me blue cocktails with umbrellas in, and oils my snake-hipped, golden-haired, nut-brown body till the sun goes down over the ocean like an exploding fireball.

That was my dream. And that was why I woke up feeling hotter than a hot towel on a long haul flight to Paradise. I was Johnny Adonis, the Greek God of beautiful bodies, and Bosie was going to fall in love with me when she saw me at The Freezer. I was too gorgeous to resist. We were going to kiss. I was certain of it.

A NOTE OF CAUTION TO MYSELF

A certainty's a wondrous thing.
It frees you up to act the king.
The only time it's not a friend,
Is when it drives you round the bend ...
By not happening.

(Johnny Casanova – writing from bitter and frequent experience)

7
THE POWER OF PRAYER

It was excellent fun while I was in it, but in the end my dream turned out to be a cruel lesson on several fronts at the same time. On the perils of being too smug, on the universal truth of the Yin and the Yang, on the balance in Nature of good and evil. It also brought me into contact with God's big joke, that amusing little phenomenon known as Sod's Law: the unwritten law that states that just when you've got your act together and for once you're feeling good about yourself, just when your life is starting to have some shape and meaning, just when you're *happy*, something ALWAYS comes along to mess you up, to make you *unhappy*, to crush your confidence and slash your emotional luggage for life.

I'll explain. When I woke up on Saturday morning I felt supreme. Let's face it, any boy who'd just killed his boring parents and then had grapes eaten off his shorts by Bosie Cricket was bound to feel a warm glow inside. I felt luckier than Elle Macpherson's pyjamas, and so it was that, with a spring in my step, I entered the bathroom to begin preparations for my date at The Freezer. I had big plans to luxuriate in lather and lotions for a couple of hours, like a Roman Gladiator before a big lion-wrestle. My *joie de vivre*, however, was soon to be cut short. I happened to glance in the mirror as I walked in, and what should have been the sweetest moment of my life turned as sour as a pint of goat sweat. There was a tiny spot on the side of my nose. I couldn't believe it. Everyone else in the world got pimples, not ME! Fourteen years of blemish-free handsomeness and now, just when I was starting my first lifetime relationship, my skin erupts in boils! Didn't God like me? First the Lada and now leprosy! I mean, didn't He approve of Bosie and me? We were a harmless, happy-go-lucky couple, not Bonnie and Clyde. It wasn't fair. It wasn't like I was asking for a perfect complexion, but middling would have been nice. The odd mildly pink skin discolouration now and then (on days when I didn't have to leave the house) would have been OK by me, but not Belisha bleepers!

I fell to my knees in front of the bidet and swore on my mother's life that I'd pray once, twice, three times a day from now on – whatever God wanted – just so long as He'd make this spot disappear.

God didn't reply. Nothing. There was a crushing, Cosmic silence. I gave a primeval cry of anguish and dashed out of the house in search of a swift and permanent cure.

ON SPOTS

Spots
Are
Not
What
Girls
Luv
Lots,
'Cause
Pus
Dis-
Gusts.

(Johnny Casanova – a.k.a. Johnny Merrick, The Elephant Boy)

"Get out," said the doctor.

"But I've grown a new head," I wailed, using subtle exaggeration to make my point.

"You're a hypochondriac."

"Then treat me for that," I said, pushing my foot through the door and bumping the doctor back against her desk. "Please, take a look," I begged. "The French Alps have just moved in on my face." I took the liberty of lying down on her couch and pulling the overhead light towards my face so she could take a proper look.

"It's nothing," she said testily.

"So you *can* see it?"

"It's just a tiny spot."

"Don't say that!" I wailed. "Lie to me. You're a doctor."

"Do you want me to lance it?" she offered, tearing the paper wrapping off a disposable scalpel. She had that nutter's glint in her eye. The one that said, *I'm mad, me. Even I don't know what I might do next.*

"Will it leave a scar?" I snivelled.

"Only a permanent one," she quipped, taking a threatening step towards me. I was up off that couch faster than a tick off a ewe in sheep dip.

"On second thoughts, maybe I'll just leave it," I grinned cheesily, as she scribbled a prescription, tore it off her pad and flicked it across the table towards me.

"Anything else I can do for you while you're here?" she enquired, taking a second step forward. "How are the muscles?"

"Bulking beautifully," I lied.

"And the testicles?"

"Oh fine," I squealed, as the steel blade swished in her hand and glinted in the light of the X-ray monitor. This doctor was a maniac. She had castration written all over her face! "I think I'll be off now," I said, slipping through the open door and slamming it shut behind me.

THOUGHTS ON VASECTOMY

Succumbing to the surgeon's knife
Will oft deny a man a wife,
'Specially if that surgeon's cuts
Remove a youthful pair of nuts.

(Johnny Casanova – pocket billiards
still played here!)

I took the prescription to the chemist, but he just laughed at me. The doctor had written "Loads of make-up" on the form. I've said it before, but I'll say it again: I am not the world's greatest fan of medical humour. In my opinion, we'd all be far better off without doctors ... unless we were dying, obviously, or needed a false leg, or had worms.

I decided to check out Mr Patel's shelves for spot cures.

"Stain Devils," he said. "This really is most popular."

"Not grease spots!" I barked.

"I am so sorry, Johnny. I am all at sevens and eights today. I am sad to admit, but my heart is no longer in my work."

"Oh dear," I said, trying to sound sympathetic when I didn't really give a monkey's. The only thing I wanted was a little bit of magic to blitz my zits.

"What I wouldn't be giving to hear the sound of a beautiful wife singing in her sari in the stockroom. Actually," he reflected, "why be fussing? She doesn't even have to be being beautiful at all."

"Very nice," I smiled. "My spot?"

"How am I supposed to be knowing?" he exploded, suddenly. "I am a shopkeeper not a pimple guru!"

"So is it noticeable?" I panicked.

"There is nothing to be seeing, Johnny. Hardly nothing at all!"

"I was thinking maybe something drastic. A purge perhaps, like they had in medieval times; leeches or a mustard poultice or red-hot tongs or something." I didn't want this spot coming back as acne. I wanted to teach it a lesson it'd never forget. Mr Patel suddenly beamed.

"Yes, I am remembering now," he said, running his fingers through his long, greying hair. "Five years ago, when I was ordering a whole gross of most ingenious turkey basters for Christmas, I was made a very special, once-only offer by the company of ten miniature turkey basters, which they had been manufacturing by some mistake in the factory. In order to get rid of these ten tiny basters, the company was renaming them Blackhead Extractors, working on the same suction principle, you see."

"Yes, I see," I said, not seeing at all. "Well, have you still got any?"

"I still have ten," announced Mr Patel. "Now where would they be?" He disappeared into his stockroom to look.

Twenty minutes later, after much banging, crashing and foreign swearing, Mr Patel emerged triumphant. "There," he said proudly, placing to his lips a small syringe with a plunger in the top, and blowing a thick, layer of dust out of the hole at the bottom. "As good as new!" I gingerly touched the thick, sticky film that encrusted it.

"So this is a turkey baster?" I said.

"No, a Blackhead Suction Pump Extractor," said Mr Patel, reading the label on the box. "For pain-free removal of pus. Quite a little marvel I should imagine. I cannot think why I have not been selling more."

"I'll take one," I said. "Can you wash it first?"

"For you, Johnny, I will even put it in a paper bag."

"You're too kind," I said.

"Only two pence extra."

When I got back home, Mum and Dad were having a barney in the garden and I ducked behind the busted Lada so they wouldn't see me. Dad had just been out to the shops and bought himself a boxful of toy soldiers, a Subutteo football game and a £50 coffee-table book on the Duke Of Wellington's most famous military campaigns.

"Why?" hissed Mum.

"War games," Dad replied. "There's no point in waging war on the neighbours if I don't have a tried and tested strategy, Babs. Look at this." He took the green felt football pitch out of the Subutteo box. "This is the battlefield. Good eh? At least it will be once I've painted a garden fence down the middle."

"If you can have war games, I want a makeover," she petitioned, pulling a dog-eared magazine out of her pocket.

"What's that?" said Dad.

"I want liposuction, Terry."

"Liposuction's for fat cats with fat heads and thighs," he told her. "You don't need it, lovely." But Mum thought otherwise.

"I've been making enquiries," she said, shoving the magazine under Dad's nose. "I want to go to this Cosmetic Surgery Clinic in Watford. And I want you to pay."

"What do you need cosmetic surgery for?" grumbled Dad.

"I'm forty years old, Terry. I look like an old paper bag. I want to be young and beautiful again."

"Buy yourself some fake tan in a bottle."

"Oh, pumpkin, please!" she simpered, putting her head on one side and rolling her eyes to look up at him. "Your ikkle love muffin only wants to be boo-kiful again. Doesn't Pinkie Perky want to play with Huffy Puffy any more?" Obviously he didn't, because Dad told her to act her age and accept the fact that he was spending his money on a state-of-the-art field gun and not his look-at-the-state-of-that wife. Then he stormed off into his shed to play generals, while Mum bit her lip and shambled back indoors. I gave it a couple of minutes (so she wouldn't think I'd overheard) before following her in.

Mum had just drained a large glass of wine when I appeared, and her sister Rene was filling it up to the top again. They both looked florid and bleary-eyed. Auntie Rene especially. She had puffy cheeks and a snotty nose and I could tell by the way she glowered at me that she wanted Mum all to herself, so she could have a good cry on her shoulder and slag off men. Ever since she'd got divorced, she never did anything else.

"Ooh, pumpkin!" squealed Mum. "You've got a little spot on your nose. Shall I give it a squeeze?" I used Dad's car to fend off her lunging fingers.

"Have you told Dad about your accident yet?" I asked loudly.

"Sssssssh!" she hissed, furiously. "It's a secret."

"This radio's gone on the blink again!" screeched Nan's voice from the sitting room. "I can't find the Home Service, Babs." Mum's eyebrows twitched like a pair of electrocuted slugs.

"Rene and I are just going to have another little drinky. Are you sure you don't want me to steam it out with the kettle?"

"No," I snapped. Then I added casually, "I won't be in tonight. All right?"

"Whatever!" she trilled, stumbling backwards and dropping into her chair.

I took my Blackhead Extractor upstairs, where Sherene was lying on the landing with my toad of a cousin, Ramone, Rene's daughter. Sherene and Ramone had a club called The Naughties But Nicies. Ramone had been all for just calling themselves The Naughties, because it sounded tough, but Sherene couldn't bear the lack of prettiness in the name, and had insisted on adding the Nicies bit to make sure people knew they were girls. Their favourite trick was to sneak up behind me and bite my bum, which was a real hoot! Only thing was, together they'd got less teeth than Nan, so it was more like a gumming. Anyway, the grim twins were blocking the top of the stairs and trying to make their lips bigger with a tooth mug.

"Look at me," said Sherene. "If I thuck hard enough, my lipth go ath crimthon ath blood and if I never take it off, they go all puffy too. I'm Pamela Anderthon."

"No you're not," I said. "For a start, you can't swim."

"Neither can you," she screamed, as I swanned past her into the bathroom to nick Dad's shaving mirror. "And you've got a rathberry on your nothe!"

"Word of advice," I sniped. "Don't ever drown near me, because I wouldn't even try to save you." Then I locked myself in my bedroom, while Sherene threw a purple rage on the carpet and Ramone opened her lungs and wailed like an American police siren.

I sat on my bed, took the miniature turkey baster out of the paper bag and inspected my facial disfigurement in Dad's mirror. People had tried to spare my feelings by telling me it was nothing, but I knew a lie when I heard one. Why was life so cruel? I was too young to be ugly. It wouldn't matter if I was old, because looks don't come into love when you're over forty – then it's just how much money you've got – but this spot was going to turn Bosie off big-time. This grotesque, mountainous lump of disease. I wanted to dig it out with a trowel! I pressed the plunger fully down into the syringe, positioned the Blackhead Extractor over the spot and followed the instructions on the box – *Pull back gently on the plunger and wait for a miracle*! – but nothing happened. I tried again, only this time I embedded the syringe in the skin surrounding the spot by constant downward pressure and drew up the plunger slowly, seeking to extract optimum suck from the vacuum pump. About halfway up I gasped for air as a seering bolt of pain exploded in my face and stabbed my sinuses. I guessed that was it, that the spot had burst, but on closer inspection all I'd succeeded in doing was suck half my cheek into the syringe. It was agony! I tugged on the pump to pull it off my face, but it was stuck fast. I turned my head upside down in the hope that gravity would release me from my torture, but the syringe just dangled there like a giant goitre. Wild horses couldn't part us. What had I done? I couldn't go to school with a turkey baster sticking out of my face! I yanked again.

"Aaagh!"

"What are you doing in there?" called Sherene, who'd been eavesdropping on the other side of the door.

"Go away," I whimpered. "No, don't! Sherene, I need your help."

"Only if you promithe to thay I'm a good thwimmer," she bargained.

"Anything," I promised, wiping the tears from my eyes and unlocking the door.

"Blimey, are you taking drugth?" she asked

open-mouthed, as she saw the syringe. I pulled her into the room.

"It's a turkey baster," I shouted. "Get it off my face!"

"But you're not a turkey," she said seriously.

"What's a baster?" asked Ramone. "Did it attack you?"

"Just take hold of the end," I cried. "No, not the plunger!" Sherene had given the plunger a tug and sucked another pound of flesh up the tube. "The syringe! The syringe!" Sherene took a firm grip of the baster, put one leg on my stomach and leaned back as far as she could. There was a gigantic *gloop!* as the Blackhead Extractor separated from my cheek. "Waaagh!" I screamed. My flesh tore and Sherene bounced back across my bed, while Ramone took advantage of my distressed condition to execute a giggly gumming. To tell the truth, I barely noticed. The spot was still intact, only now the surrounding skin was livid and red, and had swelled up like a sting from a queen bee. My vanity had created a monster! In my rage, I wrote the following notice, which I pinned up over my bed:

If I ever get another spot in my entire life, I will never, never, NEVER touch it!
THIS IS OFFICIAL!

The fury I felt at my own stupidity swiftly gave way to a blanket of suicidal depression. Solitary confinement was my only option, in a darkened room, where the world and Bosie could not see my shame.

I fell on to my bed and hugged my sightless, uncritical pillow.

"Goodbye, Bosie," I whispered, planting a tender kiss on her cotton lips.

"Goodbye, zit-face," mocked Sherene, who, unbeknownst to me, was still in the room.

"Get out!" I screamed, hurling the pillow at her head. It struck the wall with a thud and slid to the floor.

"Well," mocked Sherene, "that'th no way to treat your new girlfriend, ith it?"

WHY?

(For maximum effect please read slowly and miserably. Thank you.)

Misery is miserable,
Gloom is my twin.
I'm drowning in anguish,
How wretched my skin!

The pain stabs my vitals,
I'm plagued by despair,
By the boils and carbuncles
On looks once so fair.

Why did I do it?
Why did I baste?
I've lost my beloved
Through unseemly haste.

If only I'd left it,
Resisted the urge
To squeeze what was nothing
Until it went splurge.
If only's no use now,
I did, now I'm scarred.
Oh, Death, pay a visit
And leave me your card.

(Johnny Casanova – on a downward spiral of self-loathing)

I wanted to lie on my bed for ever. I never wanted to see the light of day again. I kept nudging the welt on my cheek to see if the inflammation had gone down, but it seemed to be getting harder, like a ball of quick-drying cement. I felt like a squirrel with a winter's worth of nuts in my cheek. I couldn't go out. It was unthinkable! On the other hand, I kept getting flashes of Bosie's tearful face on the dance floor when she realized I'd stood her up and my conscience was pricked. Leaving her to cry. That was unthinkable too! Oh God, why could I never make up my mind? I'd go. That was the answer – follow my heart. I'd go, and if things got tricky I'd come back. I'd stay flexibly mobile throughout the evening and duck out if the spot grew any bigger, or started catching the lights like a mirror ball. And then I had a brilliant idea, which propelled me out of my bed faster than a burning blanket.

I'd dress to distract. If I made my body sufficiently alluring, Bosie wouldn't be looking at my face would she? I needed something tight to enhance my natural bulges. I found an old pair of jeans which I hadn't worn since I was ten and squeezed my legs down the narrow holes. It took about fifteen minutes to roll the denim over my thighs, and fasten the waistband with a safety pin, but it was worth the effort. From the waist down I was solid like a snake. My muscles were packed in so tight they couldn't move. When I walked, I rolled my legs forward from the hip, like a man with tin legs, but in spite of the pain, I looked killer sexy with all the best bits of me on display.

On top I borrowed an orange T-shirt from Sherene, which was miles too small. It hugged my stomach and clung to my armpits like Clingfilm, cutting off the circulation to my arms. It pumped up my pecs a treat though, squeezing the muscles into taut hillocks of desire and making me look like Bruce Willis's brother. On my feet I wore unlaced Cat's, but that was it. No jumper, no jacket, no hat. I wanted the flesh visible. I needed mounds of rippling brawn to keep Bosie occupied! I did wear sunglasses though, to complete the macho image. I found an old pair of plastic "Hey-Man" shades, that I'd got off *The Beano* when I was eight, and used a bottle of Tipp-Ex to paint the letter "O" on to each ear-arm and the word Oakley between the lenses. Under disco lights nine people out of ten would mistake them for Oakley Eyejackets and if the beefy body failed, a pair of cool designer shades would be sure to distract Bosie from my spot. And so it was that I left my bedroom for The Freezer, high on the prospect of a close smoochy dance with Bosie, and, if I got lucky, maybe a sweaty snog.

8
WARM BEER IN THE FREEZER

I didn't get further than the hall before Dad stopped me.

"I'll give you a lift," he said. I think he was looking for an excuse to get away from Mum. She ran out of the kitchen looking panic-stricken. She was waving at me over his shoulder like an octopus on traffic duty and mouthing the words "Say" and "you" and "will" and "walk". I guessed she didn't want Dad taking the car out. Actually, I didn't need Mum to prompt me. Under no circumstances did I want Dad dropping me off in front of Bosie's mates in a Lada. So I said, "No thanks. Don't bother. I'm fine." But Dad was insistent and said he wanted to take the new car for a spin. "Then take it for a spin," I told him, "but not in my direction." What I wanted to say was take your crappy Lada for a spin over a cliff, but that would have got me grounded for a month. As it was, he didn't like the tone of my voice and dug his heels in.

"It's pathetic the way kids today are embarrassed by their parents. You all want to be the same," he said. I didn't want to hear this. I put my hands in my pockets and shook my fringe over my Eyejackets so I couldn't see him. "Be different, Johnny. Take a risk!" he said, punching me on the arm, right on one of Ginger's bruises. I hated it when Dad tried to be one of the lads. It sounded so false, because he'd never done anything exciting in his whole life.

"But they'll all laugh at me," I moaned.

"Then laugh back," he said, which was really sound advice if I wanted to get my teeth bashed in. "Come on." He opened the front door and dragged me out towards the car, while Mum turned a whiter shade of pale and rushed back into the kitchen to be sick.

When the front bumper hit the deck, I thought Dad was going to have a heart attack. He leapt out of the car and gawped at the mangled metal like he'd just run over the last dodo or something.

"Oh my God!" he squeaked, throwing his hands up to his head. "Oh my good God, what's happened?" Even a mushy brain like Dad's didn't take more than three seconds to put two and two together. "Babs!" His voice was quite frightening, actually. Mum appeared at the front door and smiled weakly as Dad dropped to his knees. "What have you done?" he roared.

"It must have just fallen off," she mumbled unconvincingly.

"Bumpers don't just fall off! They have to be bumped off!" Mum was shaking.

"Hadn't you better hurry, dear, or Johnny will miss his date?" But funnily enough driving me to The Freezer was no longer top of Dad's priorities.

"Not before I get an explanation!" he screamed. Mum looked more miserable than a cat in a washing machine, and was just preparing to confess when Fate took a hand, or rather Dad's twisted little mind kicked in. "Of course!" he growled. "Driver! This is all Driver's doing, isn't it?" It seemed suicidal to disagree, and Mum could certainly see the benefit in keeping quiet. Dad went ballistic, grabbed Pongo by the rim of his bucket, dragged him up the garden path, on to the pavement, through Mr Driver's gate and sat the poor, post-operative pooch on the roof of Mr Driver's car. "Peel the paintwork!" he yelled at the miserable dog. "Come on, boy, drop an acid bomb for Daddy!"

"The vet said he wasn't to overexert himself," protested Mum, but the die was cast. Mr Driver had answered the call to arms. He was standing on his doorstep with a baseball bat.

"Touch my car one more time, Worms, and I'll put yours in the Breaker's Yard." Dad accepted the challenge and redoubled his feverish massaging of Pongo's belly, which worked like a red rag to a bull. Mr Driver stormed across to the Lada and whacked a dent the size of a wok in the bonnet. This was my cue to duck out.

"Well, good luck," I said breezily. "Hope you sort it out." And I was gone. Down the front path and up the road before Dad could stop me. I leaned against a lamppost to get my breath back and heard footsteps running up behind me. Now I was for it. In the Bible, wasn't killing the eldest son the most popular means of revenge between feuding families? I had visions of Mr Driver swinging for a home run, using my head as the ball.

"Don't do it!" I cried.

"Do what?" said Sam.

"Oh, it's you," I said with an obvious sigh of relief.

"I had to get out," said Sam.

"Me too. Are you coming to The Freezer?"

"Yeah, I could do with cooling off," laughed Sam.

"Come on then," I said. As we turned out of our road, we heard a strange string of noises. It started with a smash of glass, a car alarm, and Dad shouting, "Respray!" Then there was a sound like a gas canister exploding, followed by a wet whistling and a metallic splattering like a shower of cow pats on a corrugated tin roof. Sam didn't know what it was either, but we both sure as hell recognized Pongo's howling and Mr Driver's gruff northern grunt of surprise.

Sam and I swapped parent horror stories all the way to The Freezer.

"My dad washes the window-sills." That was Sam. "And he goes round wiping fingermarks off the doors."

"Does he wear sandals with socks?" That was me.

"Yeah, and he always goes to the loo at the same time every day. Right after breakfast. With a newspaper and a lot of coughing so everyone knows not to approach the bathroom. He can't go at work, apparently. Too public."

"Mine too," I snorted. "And Mum sings when she's cooking, so all the neighbours can hear her."

"I've heard her," said Sam. "It's always Dolly Parton or Cliff Richard."

"That's all she knows," I said. "I've tried to bring her up to date, give her a crash course on modern sounds, but she can't stand Oasis or The Prodigal and she really hates The Red Hot Jelly Babies."

"Red Hot Chilli Peppers," said Sam.

"Yeah, them as well," I said, cursing my ignorance. I knew it was Chilli Peppers, I'd just forgotten, temporarily.

"And I think you'll find it's The Prodigy," added Sam with a huge grin. It was time to change the subject.

"I've never been to a nightclub before," I said.

"There's only one thing you need to know," said Sam. "Don't upset the bouncers. They're bigger than you."

"Oh, right, definitely," I said. "What's a bouncer?"

I discovered soon enough when I tried to walk past this bear in a penguin suit to get into The Freezer.

"Where do you think you're going?" he growled, catching me by the back of my T-shirt and lifting me off my feet.

"To see Bosie," I said. "I'm with Bosie." The bear laughed.

"Is she that tasty bit of wiggle with the norks?" His mate joined in with a nasal explosion of mirth that made him sound like an out of breath pig.

"She's my girlfriend," I said. I was trying to sound like I'd taken offence and he'd better retract his smut or I'd make him, but it came out more like a squeak from a dormouse trapped in the jaws of a slavering tomcat. I don't think the bouncer was that scared. He patted me on the head and hurled me through the revolving door so hard that I went round at least three times before I was spat out into the foyer. I tried to stand up, but my legs wouldn't stay straight.

"Ready?" said Sam, helping me up.

"As I'll ever be," I said, shaking out my hair and pulling it forward to cover my spot. "Let's go boogie!"

Sam wandered off for a dance with a stranger. On any other night, I'd've asked a stranger for a dance too, I mean there were about five million free girls gyrating on the dance floor, wearing tiny skirts that covered their bums like plasters, but I was faithfully waiting for Bosie. So I stood on my own on the balcony for about half an hour, scouring the sex-fest for a sight of my beloved. I was just starting to feel self-conscious when I saw her. She was dancing with some sad bloke with short black hair and a goatee beard. I could tell she wasn't enjoying herself, by the way she had her hand on the hair at the back of his neck, so she could yank his face away if he tried anything. She saw me over his ear and I waved – a secret sort of wave, an undetectable wiggle of my fingers that told her I was ready and waiting. Well, I didn't want to do one of those full-rotating upper-body waves that mums do when they meet the coach after a school trip. That would have looked too eager.

After she'd had another four dances with this bloke, who I must say was boring her to death – she practically fell asleep on his shoulder – she came over and draped herself round the pillar next to me.

"You made it," she said, raising goosebumps on my neck.

"Yeah," I mumbled. "So did you."

"Yeah," she replied. It was going well. We were talking.

"You look nice," I said, hoping she'd return the compliment, but she was gazing out across the dance floor and can't have heard me over the music. "Do you want a drink?" We wandered over to the bar and I ordered her a Coke and a beer for me. I wasn't planning to drink it – just hold it so I looked cool. It was a bit embarrassing paying for them, because I only had a pocketful of change and while I was counting out £1.46 in my hand, some large bloke in a leather jacket bumped my arm and I dropped all the coins on the floor. By the time I'd picked it all up and apologized to the growing crowd behind me, Bosie had gone back to the edge of the dance floor. "Your Coke," I said as I joined her. While she sipped there was a meaningful silence between us, during which I realized she hadn't mentioned my spot once. This filled me full of hope. "Bosie," I whispered seductively, "your father must have been a thief because he stole the stars out the sky and put them in your eyes."

"You what?" she said, putting her hand up to her ear. "I can't hear you."

"I said, your father must've been... Oh forget it." I was fighting a losing battle against the music. I just smiled at her instead.

"Are you laughing at me?" she said.

"No. I'm happy," I told her. "To be here. I like it. You and me."

"What?"

"Us." I hardly dared utter the word for fear she might reject it. "On our first date. Can I walk you home?"

"What now?"

"No, later," I said, flexing my muscles to prove I had what it takes to beat off muggers.

"I'm staying the night with Susan," she said.

"Oh right," I grieved, trying to hide my disappointment. "That's cool."

"Do you like parties?" she cut across me.

"Parties?" Blimey this was amazing. We could switch conversations in mid-flow, talk about anything. We were communicating. "I'm the original party machine," I swaggered. "I was born to party. Parties and me go together like—" I wished I hadn't started now. I couldn't think like what— "like cheese and feet."

"Good," she said, "because I'm having a rave."

"A rave!"

"Next Saturday."

"A rave!" I couldn't believe what I was hearing. A rave, that was mega-cool. That was like drugs and drink and hot dogs and things. "Where?"

"In the sitting room," she said. "12, Montpelier Crescent. Mum and Dad are going out to a bar mitzvah party and they won't be back till late."

"Don't they mind?" I gasped, imagining my parents doing their nuts.

"They don't mind because they don't know," she said, "but even if they did, it wouldn't be a problem. They're very liberal. With a small 'l', obviously."

"Obviously." I nodded wisely, with zero understanding stamped right across my face. "They sound great. I wish I could take my parents back and change them for yours."

"So will you come?" I felt that this was the moment to drop the big question.

"Are you asking me because I'm your boyfriend?" I probed boldly.

"Why do you want to know?" she shouted back.

"So that I can tell people," I beamed, excitedly. "Not that I want to rush you. If you want to keep it secret that's fine, I just personally think that other people would want to know, that's all. So they could congratulate us and give us presents."

"They only give you presents when you get married," said Bosie.

"Whoops!" I replied. "Jumping the gun a bit there!" I was laughing like a bloke who hadn't given wedlock a thought, but the truth was I'd been worrying myself sick in case we went the distance. I mean, going down on one knee to propose looked so embarrassing. Not only that, but what if I lost the ring? And what if she asked me to put up shelves? And if she accepted my proposal, she'd want curtains and a weekend in Paris. Where could I get that sort of money at fourteen? A paper round? Get real, Casanova. Tying the knot was heavy mazumba and I didn't think I was up to it.

"Look, let's get one thing clear," said Bosie. "I mean, we're both of us adults."

"Oh, absolutely," I squirmed, adding, "I've shaved eleven times now," just to hammer home my virility, but she didn't seem impressed.

"But I'm not ready for children yet."

"Me neither," I replied, nervously, hoping she didn't suddenly change her mind and discover I hadn't done it yet.

"So let's just say we're having a casual affair."

"Okey-dokey," I grinned madly. "Is kissing allowed?"

"Save it for the rave," she said, avoiding my half-hearted lunge, which I turned rather neatly into a pretend trip. "Let's dance."

There then followed the most blissful three minutes of my life. The music was loud and fast so it wasn't a clinchy sort of dance, but I kept trying to touch her by leaning forward and pretending I couldn't hear what she was saying, which brought my ear within inches of her lips.

I did quite a lot of shoulder-rubbing and backs-of-fingers brushing, and once I nearly got my hand all the way behind her back to feel that soft, fleshy bit under her arm, but I accidentally touched her bra on the way across and had to get the hell out of there in case she thought I was being rude and trying to undress her. It was dead exciting though, prodding that squidgy lump of elastic. And the smell of her sweaty hair, clinging to her shoulders like strands of wet seaweed, exuding the airprint of musty locker rooms and cheap scent – it was groin-gyratingly gorgeous.

After the dance, she disappeared and didn't come back. I felt a bit like an abandoned baby. I stood around for several minutes, fondling the bottle of beer, until I was so bored I decided to take a sip. I winced as the warm liquid sloshed over my tonsils. It had a weird taste, like sour apple juice. Ginger had told me, however, that it got better the more you drank, so I drained the whole bottle without letting it touch my throat and went back to the bar.

"Same again, chief!" I called. No please, no thank you, just "Same again, chief!" like I drank beer all the time and knew exactly how to handle it. While the barman was dealing with my order, I was knocked to the deck by a snap kick to my kidneys. It was Darren, whirling out of control, trying to impress Sharon with his hardcore dancing.

"Sorry, mate," he said. "Didn't see you standing there like a dead tree. Nobody to dance with?"

"I've just finished dancing with Bosie, actually," I said, putting him in his place.

"Feeling sorry for you, was she?"

"She was certainly feeling for me," I retorted. "We pressed flesh."

"Really?" said Darren. "So you think she fancies you?"

"I know she does," I replied frostily.

"Then you'd better go and punch him on the nose, hadn't you?" he laughed, pointing out a couple on the dance floor who were so heavily intertwined that it was impossible to tell which bit of which body belonged to who. It was Bosie and some black guy with dreadlocks.

"No. That's her brother," I said, doing a first-class job of concealing my jealousy. "Anyway, I'm not bothered, because she's asked me to a rave at her house."

"We know," said Sharon, planting a public

wet kiss on Darren's new tongue stud. "She's asked everyone in the year. We're all going, aren't we, Darren?" But the kiss on Darren's tongue stud had caused him untold agony.

"That really hurt," he cried, as she took him by the hand and led him off to the bar for an ice pack. "I think it might be infected." I hated Darren and Sharon. They were a pair of posers, who wouldn't have known what real love was if it had reached inside their rib cages and ripped out their hearts. They just did everything for show. It was pitiful.

I must admit, for the next fifteen minutes I was a bit piqued. I watched Bosie dance with a succession of men, all of whom looked older than me. They all had muscles and sideburns and cigarettes and jeans that fitted their tight butts. I hated them to death, but I still wanted to be like them. They knew instinctively what they wanted. I mean, they'd obviously wanted Bosie and had just gone and got her. Me, I couldn't even say hello without blushing. I needed to do something spectacular to attract her attention, but before I could think what, Elastic Strawberry appeared on stage, and I lost Bosie in the crowd as the girls swarmed to the front to do all that screaming stuff and chuck their knickers at the lead singer.

The blow was softened by the arrival of my second beer. I was already feeling lightheaded from the first so I knocked it back without thinking. Halfway down I started to gag. Tears streamed down my face as the warm liquid sloshed through my tubes and set off a bilious boiling in my stomach. I slammed the empty bottle down and missed the bar. The crash of glass tinkled in a far away place. The room had gone foggy. I couldn't seem to focus properly. All I could remember was that I had to let Bosie know what I felt about her. And then, as if in answer to my prayers, Cupid popped a cunning plan into my brain.

Elastic Strawberry attracted the girls like flies round a honey pot, so if I could use the band to carry my message to her, it stood to reason, she'd listen. They'd been tearing the roof off since they came on, so I was sure they wouldn't mind winding down the tempo for their final number, doing something more melodic so we could all hear the lyrics. Something romantic like a ballad. Something to melt Bosie's heart. The musical equivalent of a box of chocolates. I sidled up to the edge of the stage and swayed gently while I waited for Elastic Strawberry to finish their number – "Eat My Trouser Steak" I think it was called. It was hard to hear.

As the last power chord drifted away and the girls went crazy, I tugged the trousers of the lead singer, a nice-enough looking chap with a peroxide quiff and an eyebrow-ring the size of a parrot's perch.

"Do you do requests?" I asked, blinking hard to stop the whirling.

"No," he said, pointing me out to the rest of the band like I was some sort of alien.

"Only it's important that my girlfriend knows how much I love her, and I thought if you played a love song or something, and dedicated it to her, she might really like me."

"Get lost," said the singer. For some reason I thought he was joking.

"Thanks," I grinned as I hopped up on to the stage beside him and tugged the microphone out of his hand. "This next song," I announced, "is dedicated to the girl I love." The lead singer tried to grab the mike back. "Get off," I protested. "I haven't told you who she is yet." There were boos and hisses coming from the floor, but I didn't seem to care. I was really pumped up. "Her name's Bosie," I shouted as the singer shoved me in the back and pushed me off the stage. "Wahay! Crowd surfing!" I yelled as I flew across the heads of the girls in the first row and fell into the arms of three close-cropped thugs in leather jackets. "Howzat!" I shouted. "Well held!" They dropped me on my head. As I picked myself up I got the distinct impression I'd started something I shouldn't have. The crowd fell silent as the lead singer called for hush and I suddenly felt uncomfortably naked.

"This is for the prat," he said aggressively,

giving the drummer the nod. Then Elastic Strawberry launched into a song called "Anorak Boy", the lyrics of which went something like:

Anorak Boy, Oh Anorak Boy,
Sad little git
So give him a toy.
He lives with his mum
Who still washes his toes,
He's got spots on his bum
And spots on his nose.
He's an
Anorak Boy,
An
Anorak Boy.
A real-life prawn
And a real killjoy.

It dragged on like this for what seemed like hours. At the end, they turned a spotlight on me and the crowd had a major mock at my expense. I was paralysed with embarrassment. Then, suddenly, everything span out of control. I remember collapsing. I remember the bouncer dragging me out from under feet. I remember my mouth filling with water. I remember Sam saying, "Are you all right? You've turned grey." And I remember replying, "I don't feel vay well. Shomeone poisoned the beer!" Then it all went a bit dodgy. The club span round like I was handcuffed to the Wall of Death. I tried to lie down on the floor, but the bouncer tugged me towards the door. I was swallowing as hard as I could to stop myself from singing Hughie, but the Wall of Death had just turned into a tumble drier on spin-speed and I was panting like a hot dog in a heatwave. I felt awful. My stomach went into spasm. I told the bouncer I needed a chunder bucket, but he wouldn't believe me. I wrestled free of his grasp as we struggled through the lobby, stumbled forward, and with my hand clasped firmly over my mouth, barged past the other clubbers, crying "Sorry!" I tripped and lurched forward on to the pavement, where I scrabbled to reach the rubbish bin on the kerb before my guts blew! I didn't make it. With a contraction like a squeeze from a weight-lifter's hernia belt, my stomach rejected both bottles of beer in a multicoloured fountain that arched through the air like a wet rainbow and landed with a split-splat on the bouncer's DM's. Somewhere in the distance I heard a girl scream and then there was deathly silence. Then, through a mouthful of warm chunks, I mumbled my apologies to the bouncer and blacked out like a corpse.

I suppose Sam must have helped me up off the pavement, because it was Sam whose face I saw when I came round.

"You look rough."

"I dishgraced Bosie," I dribbled. "Gonna kill myshelf!"

"Don't be silly," Sam said. "Suicide hurts a lot more than making a fool of yourself." Which was true, but I was still allowed to wallow in self-pity, wasn't I?

STEP INSIDE MY SUICIDE

This time it's real, I'm going to do it.
Nobody stop me, my mind is set to it.
My only concern is how to obtain
The dramatic-est death with minimum
pain.
A noose when loose is of no use,
A paper-knife's too floppy.
A little blue pill only makes you ill,
A chopper's far too choppy.
You need a relation for neat
suffocation,
And ice-picks leave me colder ...
I'm thinking again
There's nothing BUT pain.
I'll die from getting older.

(Johnny Casanova – who needs the
Samaritans?)

By the time I got home, though, I'd talked myself out of the final solution. Suicide I realized was a last resort and I wasn't there yet. I was at the last resort bar one. I was at Bognor not Skegness.

9
EVERY WALLET HAS A SILVER LINING

Feeling marginally less depressed, but still seriously wobbly on my legs, I arrived home to utter chaos. The teenage policeboys were back, and Dad and Mr Driver were being arrested. Mr Driver's new car had had a respray. Gone was the shiny coat of metallic silver, replaced by splodges of greeny brown liquid that dripped off the roof and stank like a sewage plant. The Lada had a baseball bat stuck through its windscreen. Mum and Mrs Driver were helping Pongo into an RSPCA ambulance. He looked exhausted, like some giant mangle had squeezed the life out of him.

"Awright?" I cried, lurching over to Mum's side, and making a big effort not to sound sloshed. "Worr's happened?"

"Thanks for your help," Mum was saying to Mrs Driver.

"He's fair knackered, poor soul," said Mrs

Driver, patting Pongo's head. "I can't abide cruelty to animals."

"Worr's happened, Mummy?" I shouted, but Mum was still talking.

"See you later, Mrs—"

"Fanny," said Mrs Driver.

"See you later, Fanny," said Mum. "And thanks again."

"Worr's happened?" I yelled for the third time, as Mrs Driver went next door and the police car reversed out on to the road.

"Your father did a very stupid thing, pumpkin. He made Pongo explode all over Mr Driver's new car. You should have seen the fight."

"Pongo's not gonna die, is he?" I wailed, bursting into tears.

"No. He just needs restitching where his tubes have split. It was quite an explosion, even by Pongo's standards."

"Can I come out now?" came a tiny voice from the garden shed.

"Yes, Nan. The bombs are finished," said Mum. "Poor duck, thought it was the Luftwaffe," she whispered in my ear.

"You's tecking this vay calmly," I said, as she gave me her arm and helped me up the front step.

"Well, every cloud has a silver lining, pumpkin," she grinned. "I nicked your dad's wallet while the police were arresting him."

The sonic boom of Mum clattering crockery in the kitchen woke me up the following morning. For a few blissful seconds my head was full of Bosie, but then I remembered what I'd done the night before and the horror came rushing back, making my stomach plummet like a haggis down a hare hole. My mouth was as dry as a fish in a sandstorm and tasted like clogged up lumps of soiled cat litter. Mum, on the other hand, was as bright as two buttons. Sergeant Sweety had already called from the station to tell Mum that they were releasing Dad with a caution and would she like to come and pick him up. I couldn't believe it, but this was my mum's reply.

"I'll come down later, Sergeant Sweety, when I'm ready. I suggest you keep him locked up till then, and don't give him any breakfast." Then she went to Argos with Dad's wallet and came back with a turbo-charged sunlamp, which she showed off to her new friend Fanny Driver over the garden fence.

"Silly twits!" laughed Mrs Driver.

"A night in the cells will teach them a lesson," agreed Mum. "In an ideal world, Fanny, I'd have spent the money on cosmetic surgery."

"Who wouldn't, Babs? To be nipped and tucked is a woman's only pleasure these days."

"But he only had a hundred pounds in his wallet, Fanny."

"Still, the sunlamp's nice, Babs."

"You can have a go with it later, Fanny, if you like."

"Not me, Babs. I'm prone to moles."

"Best not then, Fanny," said Mum, but you could tell they liked each other by the way they kept using each other's first names to death.

When Mum fetched Dad home after lunch, he was a changed man. It was like he'd had all the stuffing knocked out of him. The wives made the husbands shake hands before they crept indoors, and a peaceful hush descended on our two houses. I suspected that Dad was suffering from a potent cocktail of shame and guilt, because when Mum showed him the sunlamp, he told her it was nice and asked her if she'd like a couple of liposuction gift vouchers for her birthday. Mum gave him a kiss and said no, he'd done enough already, and he said sorry again, for about the seventieth time in an hour.

"I tell you what I would like, though," she added, seizing the moment when Dad was at his most vulnerable, and I can't say I blamed her. "I'd like a nice little black dress, a romantic dinner for two at Gino's on Friday when the bazouki player's on, and a large bottle of Campari." As Dad nodded his head in humble compliance and wept like a baby in Mum's arms, I wished that my life could be that simple. I wished I could make it all better with

Bosie by buying her a bottle of Campari. But I suppose that's the difference between marriage and casual affairs. Marriage is a long-term commitment, whereas what I'd got with Bosie was only ever as good as the last heavy petting session. And we hadn't even had one yet!

PEOPLE CHANGE

People change for other people.
Other people change for them.
Is it true that no one living
Is a real person, then?

(Johnny Casanova – surely the most profound thing what I've ever written)

10
BOSIE SPELLS IT OUT

Monday hovered over my head like the shadow of an executioner's axe. I was dreading seeing Bosie. I rode to school with Ginger, but I wasn't in the mood for chat – I was too pensive; I was bleeding inside; I'd blown the best chance I'd ever had of getting kissed – and him being a mate, he didn't say a word. He didn't hit me either, which was a first. Then, suddenly, as we turned out of Nelson's Way, he shouted, "Look out!" A figure had leapt off the pavement into our path. I slammed on my brakes and swerved up the kerb, coming to a prickly halt in a privet hedge. Ginger was sprawled across the bonnet of a parked car, with a silver Jaguar wedged between his legs.

"Sorry," said the cause of the accident. "I only wanted a word with Johnny."

"Debra!" I yelled. "You're a loony. You could have killed us!"

"De-BORE-ah actually," she said. "I wanted to see you, Johnny. There's something I have to show you." It was Deborah Smeeton, Little Miss Metalmouth, the girl with the fixed five-bar brace, the kissing-fiend who had made my life hell while she'd been at the same school. She sidled towards me, her thick ribbed tights making a funny thrumming sound as her fat thighs rubbed together.

"I haven't got time for this," I panicked, winkling a twig out of my ear.

"They fitted my new brace on Friday," she said wetly, opening her mouth to show me. "Look, it's detachable. I can take it in and out now whenever I want." She proceeded to demonstrate, snapping it out of her mouth and holding it out for me to examine. "It's got a flesh-coloured palate this time," she laughed, as tendrils of spit dripped through her fingers, "and apparently it feels just like the real thing!" She popped it back in and ran her tongue between her lips with a salacious slurp. "Shall we give it a try?"

"You're barking," I shouted. "Get off!" But Deborah had been planning this ambush for too long to give up lightly. She pounced on top of me and pressed her lips into mine. I shut my mouth to stop her getting in, but she sucked it open and rammed her tongue inside. It was disgusting, like being kissed by a slippery slug, like having a muscle-bound worm wrapped round my epiglottis. I was choking for air. I had to breathe! In the struggle my tongue shot forward into the roof of her mouth and snagged on the wire frame of her brace. It was trapped between plate and wire, pinned like a mouse in a mousetrap! I wrenched our lips apart and the brace came away too, slurping out of her gob like a lump of bubble gum, hanging off the tip of my tongue like a dripping, pink crab.

"Yucky pukes!" I screamed. "Get it off me!" The pain was excruciating. My tongue had turned white. The wire had pierced the muscle. I could taste blood. "Debra, do something!" I gagged.

"De-BORE-ah actually," she swooned, as I turned to Ginger and screamed for help.

"You're going to need a pair of bolt croppers to cut that free, mate," he smirked. And we cycled off faster than a couple of curry-fed cheetahs.

LIFE HAS A WAY OF SPRINGING UNWELCOME SURPRISES

For years I have dreamt of my first kiss,
Imagined it blowing my mind,
With sweet, honeyed lips,
Tasting like chips,
But when it comes what do I find?

I'm punctured, I'm bleeding, I'm
speechless,
My tongue has been ripped from my
face.
My dignity ravaged,
Virginity savaged,
My tonsils De-BORE-ah's em-braced.

Is this what my life is about then?
Will all that I want never come?
Will the love that I crave
Elude me to my grave?
Will my deals for ever be bum?

(Johnny Casanova – accepting that
life is a cruel mistress with spurs on)

Bosie was, as I expected, as cold as a fish. I decided that attack was the best form of defence and tried hard all day to endear myself to her, but she wasn't having any of it. At first break, after Ginger had kindly removed the brace by levering it out with a staple extractor from the School Secretary's office, and I'd sat through French with a piece of loo paper on my tongue, soaking up the blood, I loitered in the corridor outside her classroom. When she appeared, arm in arm with Sharon, I told her I'd missed her lots, which made Sharon giggle. Bosie blushed too and ordered me to cut it out. I told her, "That's easier said than done, Bosie, because love never stops. We're riding the Great Love Snowball," but that made Sharon giggle twice as loud and Bosie ran away.

I pursued her into the dining hall at lunch and tried to be romantic by catching her eye in the queue, but Sharon's head was always in the way. Not to be denied, I pushed my way past the piddly juniors and bumped my tray into hers.

"I bet I know what you're thinking," I whispered, allowing my hand to hover just above her shoulder. This was a technique I'd developed whereby I could feel her without actually feeling her. It was a bit like warming my hands over a three-bar fire. Had I touched her, I'd have got my fingers burned.

"I bet you *don't* know what I'm thinking," she replied, casting a quick glance in Sharon's direction. I picked up the proverbial gauntlet like a mind-reader in shining armour.

"I bet you're thinking, *What's he thinking right now?* Because that's what I was thinking – *I wonder what she's thinking?* And now I bet we're both thinking, *I bet we're both thinking the same thing.*"

"I was thinking, *Shall I have chips or beans or neither and a pudding?*" said Bosie. Sharon sniggered unhelpfully.

"Oh," I said. "Do you *ever* think about me?"

"Not when you're not there," she said. "But

I think about you when I'm with you, because you never stop talking." I detected a crack in her armour. It was such a beautiful thing to say that I was moved to tell her I loved her, only the dinner queue wasn't exactly the best place to do it, what with every nosy parker in the school trying to listen in, so I just mouthed it, subtly, out of the corner of my mouth.

"What was that?" she said.

"I l... y.." I muttered imperceptibly.

"What?"

"I lurm oo," I repeated louder, opening my eyes wide in an expression of frenzied sexual ecstasy and hoping she'd get the message.

"Speak up!" By now everyone was watching. "You WHAT me?"

I tried to turn my voice into a whispering wind, blowing my words towards her like dandelion fluff, but something was irritating her.

"WHAT ARE YOU TRYING TO SAY?" she screamed, causing a funereal silence to fall over the hall. I'd have happily abandoned the whole loving moment there and then, but a thousand ears were straining to pick up my next sentence. Beads of perspiration trickled down my forehead and dripped off the end of my nose. There was nothing else for it.

"I love U2," I said.

"What?" she scowled.

"Aren't they a great band?" The clatter of knives and forks restarted.

"I hate them," said Bosie.

"Yeah, know what you mean. I can't name one of their songs. I'd have the pudding if I was you, the chips and beans are cold." She had salad just to be awkward, and when I offered to carry her tray to the table she said, "No."

Later, I tried to demonstrate my undying love by carving her name inside a heart on my desk top, but all I did was break the nib of my pen.

"Do you think it was sexist to dedicate that record to Bosie?" I asked Ginger, after I'd told him the whole sordid story from Saturday night.

"Maybe," he said.

"So you think that could be the problem? That I'm sexist."

"Yes," he replied.

"Do you spell Bosie with a 'y' or an 'ie'?" I asked.

"'Y'" said Ginger.

"Because I don't know how to spell it."

"No, you spell it with a 'Y', dimmock!"

"That's a bit of luck," I said. If it had been "ie" I wouldn't have fitted it inside the heart. There was a momentary lull as I scratched the last letter. "Only I try not to be sexist, but it's dead hard when you don't really know what it means."

"It means you shouldn't treat her like a woman," said Ginger. "I think."

"What? You mean like not opening doors, not buying flowers, and not giving up your seat on the bus even if she is twelve months pregnant?"

"That's the sort of thing," said Ginger.

"But I do that anyway," I said.

"Then you're not sexist, are you?"

"But if I carry her library books I am?"

"Probably." Being sexist or not being sexist was like walking through a minefield.

"Oi, Bosie!" I shouted into the corridor. "Get in here now and take your library books back!"

"But you offered to take them," she said, with a note of surprise in her voice.

"It's sexist," I said, handing the books over. "Aren't you pleased?" She looked a little hurt.

"Bosie is spelled with an 'ie'," she said flatly. Ginger grinned like the Devil. He'd bloody known that.

Come hometime, I couldn't bear the suspense any longer. It was the not knowing how she felt that was getting under my skin. I followed her into the locker room and told her I wouldn't let her leave till we'd had a chat. So we had a chat, her sitting on the bench and me leaning over her, with my mouth next to her ear so no-one else could earwig.

"I'm really, really sorry," I said.

"About what?" came the reply.

"About doing that tricky stuff with the

band, and getting drunk and everything."

"Oh that," she said casually. "I didn't see any of that. I was with—" she paused for the briefest of seconds— "was somewhere else."

"You didn't see any of it?"

"No."

"So you weren't embarrassed?" I couldn't believe my luck. Thirty-six hours of angst for nothing!

"Sharon told me about it later," she added, slicing my reprieve in half with a buzzsaw. I was crestfallen.

"Is that why you don't like me any more?" I asked.

"I don't not like you, Johnny."

"So why've you been ignoring me today?"

"Because you keep opening your big mouth and saying stupid things in front of Sharon."

"I don't care about Sharon," I said.

"But I do," she replied. "She's my best friend and she thinks you're a plonker. Surely you can see how difficult that makes it for me. I can't possibly tell her that I don't agree with her." Her words fell like blobs of Savlon on my raw and tortured soul.

"You mean you like me?"

"Yes. No. I mean, you *are* a plonker, but not as big a one as all the other boys in the school. Besides you make me laugh, and if you were to change certain things about yourself, I think I could like you lots."

"Change?" I said quickly. "Which bits?" Bosie told me to sit down beside her.

"Well, since you've asked," she said, "I've got a list, and no interrupting. I like well-built sporting heroes, especially anyone who does judo, because they can protect me on the bus."

"I'm in the swimming team," I protested, silently cursing Ginger for you-know-what.

"You said you wouldn't interrupt," she said sharply. "This is important to me. Number two, I'm partial to New Men."

"Well, I'm fairly new," I said. "I'm only fourteen years old."

"New as in modern," she tutted. "I like a man to pull his own weight in a relationship. Not only must he be tender and attentive, but he's also got to be practical around the home and do all the cooking and washing up without waiting to be asked."

"Is that all?"

"No, he should be kind to pets and old people, as well."

"I am," I said. "Farty old dogs and batty old grans a speciality!"

"You're still interrupting," she said.

"Sorry."

"Intelligent, artistic and a writer of songs would be nice. And you have to wash that horrible hair."

"Horrible? It's designer grunge!"

"And if you're ever going to go out with me

properly, you'll have to get a tattoo on your bottom, as a mark of your commitment."

"Isn't that painful?" I said.

"Very," said Bosie. "Especially when the needle's blunt."

"Blimey, you don't ask much, do you?" I said, after I'd caught my breath. "You only want me to change absolutely everything about myself."

"You won't regret it," she glowed suggestively.

"So let's get this straight," I back-tracked. "You want a muscle-bound hunk with a heart of gold? A rock and roll god with the brain of Magnus Magnusson? A caring, sharing, cooking man with a tattoo? And you want me to wash my hair?"

"That's about the strength of it," she confirmed.

"And if I change into this perfect man, will you love me?"

"I didn't say I'd love you," she teased. "I said I'd let you be my date at the rave and maybe – just maybe – kiss me." That sounded like a fair swap to me, so I agreed.

To the untrained eye it might have looked like I was the one making all the sacrifices, but I had just seen Dad give in to Mum, and look where that had got him? Back in her good books, a bosom to cry on and God knows what else besides (once Sherene and I were out of the house). My family and neighbours were living proof that change was for the best. I'd struck a good deal. Bosie and I were very nearly a unit, which gave me a nice, warm feeling in my pocket. I may have been imagining it, but when I was using the urinal a couple of minutes later, I was pretty sure that the boy standing next to me was sneaking a look at my little fella, to check out what made me so special!

11
ALL CHANGE

I had to get myself organized. It was Monday night. I had five days till Bosie's rave, which gave me just one hundred and twenty hours to transform myself from an unattractive teenager into a beefcake in rubber gloves. I planned out my schedule. Tuesday I'd get fit in the gym, collar Ginger for a judo lesson and invite Bosie to dinner on Friday when Mum and Dad were having their tête-à-tête at Gino's. Wednesday I'd take Pongo and Nan into school to demonstrate my care for pets and the elderly, leaving the evening free to pop along to the funfair on the common and get a tattoo. Thursday I'd wash my hair and write a love song, and Friday I'd learn to cook. That left Saturday morning free to indulge my body in lotions, potions and sweet-sweet notions for my night of passion with Bosie. Whichever way I looked at it, it was a full week.

I enrolled myself into the local gym on Monday night and was told to turn up at seven o'clock the following morning for a fitness assessment test with Bill the supervisor. Unfortunately, I never got further than the changing room. You should have seen the size of those weight-lifters. Lumps of meat all over them! Huge, glistening pecs like jellyfish. I wasn't taking my clothes off in front of them. No way. Next to them, I'd have looked like a stick insect with anorexia! So that none of them would think I was chickening out, I slung my gym bag over my shoulder, and said loudly, so that everyone could hear, "Catch you in a mo, guys. Left my isotonic drink and tube of steroids in the car. Just going to get them. Make sure you save the heaviest piece of equipment for me, OK?" And then as I was walking out. "God, don't you just love pumping iron!" You know, I don't think any of them guessed I was running away. That's because body-builders are so thick.

Ginger was less than supportive when I told him my plan and how he fitted in. He thought I shouldn't change a thing about myself or I'd end up like Sharon and Darren, and that Bosie was a bit weird in the head for asking. I told him he was just jealous, because Bosie was all woman and he needed two girlfriends to match up to my one.

"The twins are not my girlfriends,"

protested Ginger. "They might want to be, but they're not."

"So who is then?" I asked.

"I don't know," sighed Ginger. "I can't see the wood for the trees at the moment. Apart from the twins, there's Mandy who babysits my brother; Tricia; Sally; Charlotte; that girl with the long fringe in Biology, what's her name ... set the frogs free ... Alex, that's it; my second cousin Rebecca and that rather lovely girl down the chip shop. I can't pronounce her name."

"This is a wind up," I gasped.

"No," said Ginger. "They just seem to like me, that's all."

"This *is* a wind up."

"It's not, but it does prove one thing, that I'm not jealous of you. Besides, I'm more interested in Bernard."

"Oh yeah!" I sniggered, suggestively.

"Because of judo. Thanks to Bernard, I've got my life in perspective. I'm 'maintaining my unity'."

"I don't believe this," I said.

"It's the T'ai Chi. Bernard says that maintaining unity brings good luck. Examine the primal cast for eternal steadiness, he says. It is not at fault. The restless come from afar, and disaster befalls the late husband."

"Bow-locks!" I said. "Disaster will befall you if you keep listening to that twaddle!"

Ginger shrugged. "So what do you want me to do?"

"Teach me to be a black belt," I said.

"That takes years," he said.

"I've got till school starts," I told him, which made him laugh, but I couldn't see what was funny.

"That's only twenty minutes," he snorted, "And where's your judogi?"

"At the vet's, having his tubes restitched,"

"It's a judo suit," Ginger explained wearily.

"Oh," I said. "Couldn't you just show me a few moves?"

"All right," he sighed, "but first you've got to promise me you'll do whatever I tell you to." I didn't like the sound of that at all, but I didn't have much choice, so I agreed. "Right, fall over!"

"On the playground? I'll break my arm!"

"We'll go over there, then," he groaned, "where there's some grass." It wasn't grass, as it happened, it was a mud bath.

"You must be joking," I grumbled. "I'll get covered."

"Forget it, then." Ginger turned his back and walked away.

"All right, all right!" I shouted, stopping him in his tracks. "Like this?" and I threw myself head first into the bog, splattering my blazer and hair with cold slime. "Satisfied?" I said cheerlessly.

"That was hopeless," he grinned.
"You're enjoying this!" I fumed.
"Only quite a lot!" he sniggered. "You've got to learn how to break your fall with your arms." He showed me what he meant and made me practise it several hundred times until I looked more peaty than the creature from the Black Lagoon.
"Can't we do some throws?" I complained.
Ginger took a pace forward, grabbed my right arm and twisted me over his right shoulder.
"That's an ogoshi," he said.
"That's bloody painful," I groaned, lying on my back with the wind knocked out of me. "You've yanked my arm out of its socket. Can I try it on you?"
"No," said Ginger, "we've got company."
It was Miranda Bletchley from the sixth form. Her mum organized rock concerts, which made her the most popular girl in the school. She was gorgeous too. Looked like a super-model only shorter.
"I've done your History essay, Ginger," she said. "Do you want it now or shall I give it to you after school?"
"I'll take it now. Saves trouble later."
"Oh it's no trouble," Miranda said. "I was going to ask you if you wanted to go for a coffee later, anyway."
"Sure," said Ginger. "Whatever. Thanks for doing the essay."

"My pleasure," she smiled. "I'll see you by the bus stop, then. Bye." I was catching flies as I watched Miranda walk away.

"Miranda Bletchley!"

"Yeah, I forgot about her."

"How did you get Miranda-gimme-the-raging-horn-Bletchley to do your history for you?"

"She offered," said Ginger. "Now, am I teaching you judo or what?"

"I've had enough," I said. I was heavily depressed.

"All right, but let me show you one more move before you go," he said, sweeping his right leg into the back of my knees and felling me like a tree. The next thing I knew I was back in the mud again and Ginger was roaring with laughter.

ON JUDO

If Ginger ever tries again
To put me on the deck,
I'll seoinage his ippon
And break his bloody neck!

(Johnny Casanova – rei-ing out of
Martial Arts for good!)

The upshot of Ginger's judo lesson was that when I approached Bosie to ask her over for dinner on Friday, she wrinkled up her nose and said I looked like a mudlark and my hair smelled even more revolting than last time. She made me stand on the other side of the corridor before she'd talk to me.

"So will you come?" I said. "I mean, obviously if you don't want to meet my family, you don't have to. Not that you will have to, actually, because Mum and Dad are going out, and you've met Mum anyway – voice like a bat with a loudhailer, remember? But you will have to meet my little sister Sherene and she's a mega-pain." The trick was to keep speaking so she couldn't get a word in. I didn't want to give her the chance to say no. "And Pongo's supposed to be a dog, but he's more like a leaky lilo full of fart gas. Just so you know." She opened her mouth to speak. "And our house is on an estate. It's quite big, with a garden and a shed, but it's not old." Bosie coughed. "Forewarned is forearmed," I explained. "And my bedroom's tiny and I've still got a poster of Claudia Schiffer on the wall, but I don't fancy her. I got given it at Christmas. She doesn't mean a thing to me."

"I haven't said I'll come yet," she said calmly.

"I wouldn't bother," I said, hoping that she'd disagree and tell me there and then that she'd come. But she didn't. "I mean, Nan's away with the fairies. You have to humour her or she wets the bed, because of the doodlebugs, and we don't eat caviar, although I'm pretty partial to it myself. We're more of a corned beef, Spammy sort of a family. Common as muck you'd probably call it."

Bosie was checking her watch. "I'm not boring you, am I?" I was acutely conscious that I was doing all the talking, but somebody had to fill the silence, and I'd read in *SKY* magazine that boyfriends were expected to take the driving seat in matters conversational. Now I'd done it. I'd tempted Fate by thinking the word boyfriend! Now she'd definitely say no. "Shall we say seven o'clock?"

"Seven o'clock," said Bosie.

"Very funny," I snorted. "So you'll come?"

"Watch this space," she said. I couldn't believe it. It wasn't a yes, but it definitely wasn't a no!

The next day Pongo was still under the knife, so my love of animals demonstration had to wait. As far as helping the aged, I managed to convince Nan to accompany me into school by telling her that Winston Churchill was singing "White Cliffs of Dover" at our assembly. I nicked a wheelchair out of the hospital car-park and wheeled her to the bus stop where Bosie got off the bus every morning. I put dark glasses on her face, a rug over her knees, and told Bosie that she was blind and couldn't walk – to pump up the importance of my good works, you understand. Then I force-fed her a Mars bar and said it was Meals on Wheels, but Bosie was not impressed, especially when Nan leapt out of the chair and hopped on the bus, shouting, "Take me to the Anderson Shelter! There'll be powdered eggs for tea!"

Next up was the tattoo. I didn't sleep a wink the night before with worry. A tattoo was for life, but what if Bosie didn't last that long? Unless I lost my buttock in a bizarre squatting accident with a bacon slicer, I'd be a marked man till the day I died!

ON WHY LUV HURTS AND
TATTOOS TOO

Ooh! Ooh! Tatty tattoo.
Needles and ink,
A gangrenous stink.
Ooh! Ooh! Tatty tattoo.
Opening a vein
Would cause me less pain.
Ooh! Ooh! Tatty tattoo.
I'd give it a miss
If it weren't for a kiss.
Ooh! Ooh!
Boo-hoo!

(Johnny Casanova – why did I
ever agree to this?)

After school, Sherene got wind of the fact that I was going to the funfair and insisted on coming too. This meant I'd have to find some way of losing her for twenty minutes, while I went inside the tent belonging to the Bearded Lady, who, according to the sign outside, also did *Tattoos While U Wait*.

"What are you doing?" asked Sherene.

"It's a secret," I said. "Go away."

"Well it'th not that much of a thecret," she replied. "You're either going in there to get a tattoo or to learn how to grow a beard." That made her snicker.

"Here's a pound to get lost in the maze," I said, chucking her a coin. "And remember, you didn't see me do this."

"Yeth I did," I heard her say as I pushed my way through the flaps. It was dark inside. A candle flickered on a round table in the centre of the red tent. At the back, against the canvas wall, hung a long, sparkly dress. Probably Ms Furry Freak's I thought. There was a long wig dangling off the back of a chair, but no sign of a lady, bearded or otherwise.

"Hello," I called.

"What do you want?" rumbled a deep, throaty voice. I took a step back as a huge, leather-clad Hell's Angel burst through a flap in the wall. "We're closed," he growled, shoving his long, black beard into my face. I was terrified. Hell's Angels bit the heads off live chickens, didn't they?

"I'm looking for the Bearded Lady," I peeped.

"She's out."

"Oh." That kiboshed that then. "Do you know when she'll be back?" I asked. "Only I need a tattoo done urgently." The Hell's Angel picked a piece of white flesh from between his stumpy, brown teeth. The sound of strangled clucking flashed through my brain!

"I'll do it," he grunted.

"Thank you, but I'd prefer the lady."

"I've already told you. She's not here and she's not coming back neither!" A horrible thought suddenly struck. He hadn't killed her had he? He did look a bit strange. His fingernails were painted pink. "Strip to the waist."

"I want a heart or something. It's got to be romantic."

"How about a spitting rattlesnake coiled around a bloody dagger?"

"Sounds perfect," I said. I was too scared to argue.

"Good choice," he thundered. "That's on special offer." He walked across the tent to a wooden cabinet and rummaged around inside. "This your first time?" he asked, turning round with a bag of spiky tools in his hand – probably the murder weapons. I nodded nervously, unsure whether to concentrate on the instruments of torture or the gold stiletto shoes that were poking out from under his ripped jeans.

"The only thing is—" I stammered, laughing nervously— "erm ... I don't want it on my arm."

"Oh?" he said, unrolling his bag of fun.

"My girlfriend wants it down below."

"Down Belows are extra," he said bluntly, slipping the diamanté earrings off his ears.

"How much?" I gulped.

"Depends how much pain you want," he smiled, sandpapering the rust off his longest needle.

"Absolutely none," I squeaked, suppressing nightmare visions of this man-monster hacking the bearded lady to death.

"Then manual it is," he leered, "and sixty quid!"

"Sixty quid!" Fear or no fear I couldn't pay that. "I've only got a fiver!" The Hell's Angel wiped the back of his hand across his lips and smeared it with lipstick.

"Then we'll have to come to some arrangement, won't we?" he snarled, pulling a large chisel out of his back pocket. I don't remember what followed. I must have blacked out. The next thing I knew I was lying in the dirt outside the tent with a pain in my backside that hadn't been there ten minutes earlier.

"Well, it can't have been a beard, becauthe you're ththill peachy," said Sherene. "Tho where'th the tattoo?"

"He's a murderer," I whispered, hoarsely. "He's killed the Bearded Lady!" Sherene clocked the Hell's Angel as he slipped out of the tent and walked across the field towards the road, wearing the long, sparkly dress.

"He doethn't look very dangerouth to me," she said dismissively. "He'th got a handbag."

"He's stolen her clothes!" I explained.

"You're making it up," said Sherene. "You're trying to thcare me, becauthe you don't want me to tell Mummy."

"Too right I don't," I said. Half an hour in a tent with a psychopathic cross-dresser was infinitely preferable to telling Mum I'd got a tattoo. She'd go mental.

My bum was still bruised as we walked home. Sherene seemed to find it amusing.

"What is it?" I said, irritated by her giggling.

"I wath thinking how funny it ith. You get a tattoo to make your girlfriend happy, tho thhe'll kithth you, but if thhe doeth kithth you and doeth grab your bottom, you will jump through the roof. Tho, NO kithth!"

"Promise you won't tell Mum," I begged.

"What'th it worth?" she smiled. I could see her devious little mind clicking away behind her eyes.

"No," I said. "That's not fair."

"I want to thee it!"

"No. It's private, Sherene."

"I will tell Mummy. I will!"

"All right! Wait. Maybe."

"Maybe?"

"Definitely," I sulked. When Sherene grew up, she was going to work for the Mafia – blackmail and boxed-ears department.

At home, Mum had picked up Pongo from the vet's. He was lying half-dead on the kitchen floor. In addition to the blue bucket, he was now wearing a rubber nappy. It was the only thing Mum could think of to protect her soft furnishings. We stepped over him and went straight up to my bedroom, where I showed Sherene what the Hell's Angel had painted on my bum.

"That ith dithguthting!" she retched. "What ith it?"

"It's a *B* for Bosie."

"Or Bottom," sniggered Sherene. "It lookth like you're marking bitth of your body in cathe you forget what they're called. *H* for head, *A* for appendix..."

"I get the joke," I said.

"*T* for toe."

"It was all I could afford."

"*N* for nose. *K* for kidleys. *W* for wee-wee."

"Thank you, Sherene."

"*TH* for thtomach..." She'd have gone on all night if I hadn't shoved her in the C for cupboard and thrown away the *K* for key.

ALPHABETTI BOSETTI

Our luv's like a letter,
The letter is B.
B for Byronic
And on Bended Knee.
It's also for Blowing
A kiss on the Breeze
And for Birds, Bosie,
Birds...
Listen!
Birds and for Bees!

(Johnny Casanova – fly to my nest on Saturday night, Bosie, and let's make sweet honey)

With the acquisition of the tattoo I turned the final bend and entered the home straight. The worst was over. I was now of the belief that Bosie and I had a real chance. That maybe, one day, we'd be surrounded by four fat children in our sunshine home, looking back on this tattoo as the thing that got it all started. There again, maybe one day, I'd be sitting alone in my flea-ridden bedsit, surrounded by a grubby duvet and a map of the London Underground System, looking back on this tattoo as the thing which gave me blood poisoning. That's the wonder of life, though. You just don't know what it's got in store, do you?

I released Sherene for supper and wished I hadn't. She swore she'd get me for locking her in the cupboard and lost no time in telling Mum how cruel I'd just been to her, and how she could have suffocated, and how I had a sore bottom from getting a big bearded man who was also a woman to carve a tattoo into my skin with a knife.

Mum's ears pricked up sharply. "What tattoo?" I could have kicked the chair out from under Sherene. Mum hated tattoos more than she hated blokes with hairy backs and nipple studs. Tattoos were common, pornographic skin paintings, fit for sailors and Bovver Boys.

"A TATTOO!" She disappeared under the kitchen sink and reappeared with an orbital sander. "WHERE?"

"No, Mum! I did it for Bosie. She likes that sort of thing, and I've got to keep it. It's my only chance of kissing her!"

"WHERE?"

"On the lips," I said, before I realized what she meant.

"It'th on hith bottom," announced Sherene, "I'm the only one who'th theen it!"

"Bend over," Mum ordered, plugging the sander in.

"Mum..." But she was tugging at my belt, and Pongo, thinking it was a game, had sunk his teeth into my trousers and was trying to drag them across the floor. The top button burst with a twang and my legs were stripped bare.

"There," squealed Sherene. "There it is. I told you he'd got one." Mum's face exploded.

"Stay still," she cried. "I'm going to sand it off!" I twisted out of her grip and fell to the other side of the kitchen, as she plunged the electric sander into the table and gouged a lump out of the wood. "Right," she yelled, "get your coat, young man!" Which is how come I ended up back in the doctor's surgery for the third time in as many weeks.

"What is it this time?" sighed the doctor wearily.

"I want you to remove this!" seethed my Mum, whipping down my trousers to reveal my Bosie brand.

"Remove what?" queried the doctor.

"This tattoo," explained Mum, taking a closer look. "Well, it was here a minute ago."

"Mrs Worms, what is it with your family? Don't you think I've got better things to do with my time than be the butt of your practical jokes?" The tattoo had disappeared. Sherene found it on the floor, curled up like one of those plastic fortune fishes you get in Christmas crackers. It was a transfer. Now it was my turn to let off steam.

"Bloody hell," I said. "It's not real. What a

swindler! That thing cost me a fiver!" and I stormed out into the waiting room, forgetting that I still had my trousers round my ankles.

It was the end of the second day of my makeover and I had achieved zilch. No muscles, no judo, no Brownie points for helping the aged and no tattoo. A right useless lover I was turning out to be. Being Bosie's ideal man was harder than it looked, and the way my luck was running, tomorrow, when I washed my hair, I'd probably pick up a bottle of sulphuric acid by mistake!

Actually, the hair wash turned out to be my first major success. By seven o'clock the following morning, I'd dirtied three towels, left a black ring round the bath, and finished both bottles of Mum's best salon conditioner. At first, I didn't realize I was meant to rinse it out and ended up with hair that was twice as greasy as when I'd started, but once I'd read the instructions it got sorted. I finished up with hair so full of volume, with roots so nourished and split ends so tangle-free, that I could have walked on to any set for a shampoo commercial and got the job of chief hair-twirler.

After the grooming, I lavished attention on the artistic side of my character. I went down to Mr Patel's shop to buy a guitar. If I was going to compose a love song for Bosie, I was going to need something to play it on.

"I have a little one," announced Mr Patel,

which probably explained why he didn't have a wife, I thought.

"Oh, guitar," I said, as he bent down and produced a small, triangular cardboard box from under the counter. He slid off the lid and took out a ukulele. "That's not a guitar," I said firmly.

"Oh, yes, a guitar, that is right. For beginners. That is why it only has four strings." The shop bell rang and Ginger walked in to get his dad's paper.

"What are you doing here so early?" he asked.

"He is making to buy a most beautiful guitar," said Mr Patel.

"That's a ukulele," said Ginger. "My guitar's much bigger than that."

"It is cut down, for little fingers," said Mr Patel, who was desperate to shift his dead stock. "Three pounds only," but I'd lost interest. Why pay for an instrument when I could get one free?

"Ginge," I said. "Mate. It's really lovely to see you."

"You're not borrowing my guitar," he said sharply.

"Oh, go on," I begged him. "Just till Saturday."

"But you don't play," said Ginger, picking up a copy of *The Mirror*.

"I do," I lied. "We could go and get it now."

Ginger hesitated. "I thought we were supposed to be best mates," I wheedled. The guilt card was always the best in the pack.

"I'll kill you if it gets broken," he said. "It cost me three car washes and an afternoon lugging horse manure."

"I'll treat it like it was my own," I promised.

"That's what I'm worried about," said Ginger, tucking the paper into his pocket absent-mindedly.

"Come on, then," I said. "Let's go." Mr Patel coughed.

"Mr Ginger, sir. That will be thirty-six pence only," he said.

"*He's* paying," said Ginger, stabbing his finger into my chest. "He owes me."

Ginger's guitar was a monster. A red and white Falcon with a whammy bar and three white knobs. The amplifier was a Big Boy DGX45, which Ginger assured me was state of the art. It looked a bit pathetic to me. I was expecting a towering, stainless steel, heavy metal stack, but the Big Boy DGX45 was only thirty centimetres tall and had a cardboard back. Still, it made a horrible noise when I got it back to my room after school, which was all that mattered. He'd also lent me a book called *Wayne Tinsel's Teach Yourself Rock Guitar*, which was fairly essential as I couldn't play a note. I locked the door and started to practise by following the chord diagrams at the back.

It was a lot harder than I'd thought it was going to be. Five minutes after I'd started, my shoulder ached from stooping to read the instructions on the floor. After six minutes of pressing down on the steel strings, the finger-tips on my left hand felt like I'd slit them with razor blades. After ten minutes they were bleeding all over the carpet, and after fifteen minutes I'd used nearly two boxes of tissues to staunch the sticky flow. I had, however, mastered the chord of E. At least, I'd mastered the left-hand finger positions, but strumming was altogether more tricky. Wayne Tinsel instructed me to use the back of the fingers on my right hand, but I kept snagging them on the strings and chamfering little bits of skin off the top of my knuckles. A little stack of skin flakes piled up on my knee, like a mound of grated cheese. So I did away with Wayne and invented my own technique of striking the strings with my nails, which was fine on the down strokes, but sheer bloody agony on the way up when I ripped all my nails out.

By midnight I'd added chords D, F and A to my rock and roll repertoire, but I was too knackered to write the love lyrics. I decided to get up early and write them before I went round to Bosie's house to serenade her. Then I crawled into bed, where I fell asleep instantly and dreamed I was Jimi Hendrix sitting in stocks having my hands gnawed off by a pot-bellied pig.

I got up at four and dashed off the lyrics in my notebook. The house was freezing. My breath smoked as I crept downstairs and tiptoed through the kitchen. I slid Pongo's bottom across the floor to open the back door, but my touch set him off like a bomb with a tilt detonator, and he seeped a smoggy squeaker out of his singed and smoking seat. It dripped down the back of my throat like a warm, wet cup of raw sewage. Mind you, it thawed out my vocal cords a treat. I was in fine voice as I pushed Dad's wheelbarrow down the side path into the carport where the Lada was parked. I needed the battery to power the Big Boy amp. Once I'd removed it from the car and balanced it on the wheelbarrow, along with a set of jump leads and the musical doings, I set off on the thirty-minute walk to Bosie's house and ran through my lyrics at full volume, until a policeman in a panda car pulled up alongside me and asked me if I was a burglar.

"No," I said. "A lover, on a mission to woo." And he let me off with a mocking laugh and a caution.

Montpelier Crescent was dead posh, and the driveways were full of those monstrous, 4-wheel drive, off-road jeeps that rich mums find so essential for popping six metres down the road to block the traffic outside schools. Thank God I wasn't in Dad's Lada. It would have stuck out like a sore thumb on a hitch-hiker.

It was about 6 o'clock by the time I'd connected the amp to the battery with the jump leads. The Crescent was still asleep as I plugged in the guitar and tuned up. I wasn't actually sure what an in-tune guitar should sound like, but I got all the strings sounding nearly the same and decided that would do. Then I picked a shrivelled red rose from next door's front garden and scooped up a handful of gravel from the drive, which I lobbed at what I thought must be Bosie's window. The stones clattered against the glass. I held my breath and waited. Then there she was. Her soft silhouette came to me through the curtains as she switched on her light and peered outside. I turned up the gain on the amp, placed the red rose between my teeth, stepped backwards into the light of the streetlamp and strummed my opening chord. Her curtains shot open, her window shot up and her mouth shot off.

"What are you doing?" she hissed.

"Sewenading you," I mumbled, checking my finger positions and hitting my second chord. The rose made speech tricky. The thorns had embedded themselves in my gums and wouldn't come out. It was like having a porcupine in my mouth as I sang:

You've got really nice hair,
And I-ya love you-s.
I like most of your socks,
'Cause they ma-a-tch your shoes.
You're the nicest girl
In the whole wide school,
Won't you let me please
Be-he your fool ...
In love!
Yeah!
I jester wanna be your fool ...
In love!
Yeah!
Bosie Cricket's fool in love!

The song went on like that for pages, going round and round in circles, because that was all I'd had time to write. Unfortunately, I was standing too close to the amplifier. The feedback from the guitar howled like a ruptured wolf and drowned out my honeyed voice. Bosie gawped in disbelief (or was it admiration?) as I fumbled the chords and crooned like Pavarotti's tomcat, causing lights to snap on up and down the street.

"Shut up!" came a sleepy cry from next door, as I poured my soul into the lyrics and crescendoed on the soppy bit that mentioned her name.

"I lub yer," I called out in one of the gaps between chord changes.

"Go away!" shouted the voice, but I hadn't come all this way to sneak off with my tail between my legs, besides Bosie was smiling. I think she was genuinely moved. I launched into the chorus again, because that was the bit I was best at, just as the neighbour appeared in his pyjamas.

"It is six o'clock in the morning!" he roared, producing a black bucket from behind his back.

"I lub her," I said.

"And that's my rose!" He tore it out of my mouth, slashing my gums to ribbons.

"Waaaaaaaaah!" I wailed.

"So you *can* sing in tune," he said snidely. "Now, disappear!"

"But I haven't finished yet."

"You have now," he snarled, swinging the bucket behind his back and letting fly with a gallon of cold water. It hit me full in the face and deluged the battery at my feet, short circuiting the sound system by shooting a fizzing blue spark along the jump leads, into the amp, and out through the jack plug into Ginger's guitar. My song squelched to a halt as I quietly exploded. I stood and dripped, my singing curtailed, my fingers blackened from the shock, a wisp of white smoke mushrooming upwards into the trees like a Pongo-parp special.

"Well?" I said, grinning through the pain. "Are you coming?"

"Where?" she replied.

"To dinner tonight. I've washed my hair."

"Has anyone ever told you how cute you look when you're wet and electrocuted?" she said.

"Frequently," I called up. "So are you coming?"

"Is Romeo asking?"

"No, it's me, Johnny," I said. "You probably can't see that well, because it's dark."

"I was making a reference to Romeo and Juliet," she sighed. "On the balcony."

"Oh yeah," I said. "That's Shakespeare, isn't it?" Bosie nodded.

"Yes, all right. I'll come. And I might even bring that kiss with me." I could hardly believe my ears.

"You mean … tonight?" I screamed. "Yahoo!"

"Keep your voice down," she hissed. "And come half an hour early on Saturday, before everyone else."

"So we can be alone?" I simmered sexily.

"So you can help me move the furniture," she whispered. "Quick! You've got to go. My parents are coming."

"They won't mind," I ventured bravely. "You said they were liberal with a small 'l'."

"They're also tired with a small 't', which makes them grumpy with a big 'G'."

"Got you!" I said, as Bosie slammed shut her window. It was time to go. I bundled the charred remains of my serenade into Dad's wheelbarrow and scooted up the road, faster than a market gardener with a mole in his moleskin trousers.

It was only after I'd reconnected Dad's car battery, that I truly came to terms with the enormity of what had just occurred. Bosie loved me. Nothing else in the world seemed to matter.

ON WHAT DOTH MAKETH
A WENCH SEXY FORSOOTH

It striketh me that a serenade
Doth putteth the oyster in the shade.
For wheneth push doth come to shove,
Making music best maketh luv.

(Johnny Casanova – thy wilst most probably hath noticed the influence of the Shakespearean bard in mine work, forsooth, sirrah, which doth verily cometh from mucheth reading of the tragedye called *Romeo and Juliet*)

12
BURNT BEANS AND FROSTBITE

Over the next few hours my love blossomed like a cheese plant. I say that because Dad's got one in the sitting room that's growing so fast you can't see the telly for fronds. As I got ready for school, I indulged in a harmless game of vanity, speculating on what it was that Bosie found magnetically attractive about me. My height was improving, I had lovely lanky hair, I dressed like a CK model, I still had my own teeth and, probably the clincher, I was completely spot-free. Since the horror of last weekend I'd changed my approach to God, and it was working. Gone were the long prayers in soppy Bible-speak (wherefore if thou dost rent my visage with tongues of fire, I will be most comely, oh powerful one – that sort of stuff) and in came to-the-point statements of fact in plain English: Dear God, I know I'm not your best disciple, but if you keep the spots away I promise I'll be full of faith from now on, and not just at Christmas! Then I shut my eyes real tight and imagined the Holy Spirit cleansing my pores with his wand. In truth, when I boiled it all down, I decided that Bosie just loved me for who I was! I went down to breakfast with Cupid's wings fluttering on my back and wandered into the kitchen in a dream. I was willing the day to flash past, so that tonight's dinner would come quicker, and then it would be Saturday, when me and my girlfriend would dance groin to groin by the sexy light of a forty-watt fireglow bulb.

DIVINE INTERVENTION

Dear God make me handsome,
Dear God clear my zits,
Dear God make me Mr Sex
Whom girlies luv to bits.
Dear God give me Stussy,
Dear God style my hair,
Dear God make me perfect,
Then I'll know that you are there.

(Johnny Casanova – I must be one of God's chosen children, being as how my skin is now as soft as a baby's bottom)

I'd read somewhere that the best chefs were

the ones who planned ahead. So I told Mum straight away what was happening.

"You've got a girl coming round for dinner tonight?"

"Bosie," I said.

Mum leaned over the table and rustled Dad's newspaper. "Our little Johnny's got a girlfriend!" she twittered excitedly.

"Got a girlfriend what?" muttered Dad suspiciously.

"Just got a girlfriend, Terry. Isn't that wonderful?"

"I'm in heaven," grunted Dad.

"Oh, Johnny, I'm so happy for you," beamed Mum. "I can remember when I first met your dad. He was that handsome he gave me goosebumps in all my unmentionables!"

"I'm very pleased to hear it," I said, feeling slightly sick, "but I just need some help with the food."

"Don't worry, I'll cook you your favourite," said Mum, still beaming.

"No, you don't understand," I said. "I knew this would happen. It's sweet of you to offer, but I've got to do the cooking myself. That's part of the deal."

"Oh, I get it," winked Mum. "She's one of these feminists is she? Burned her bra in kindergarten."

"Something like that," I sighed. "Can you help?"

"Let's see what we've got in the freezer."

In the freezer we had a chicken, several shrivelled fish fingers, a packet of peas, three ice-pops, a plain pizza, a plate of cooked tripe and Sherene's Barbie doll, the loss of which had caused the family rumpus that led to the discovery of Uncle Philip's prostate problem.

"So what do you think?" I asked Mum.

"You're the chef, pumpkin," she said, handing me a dog-eared copy of *Delia Smith's Winter Collection*. "Have a look through that." Sadly, Delia did not have a section entitled "Cooking For First Time Morons Who've Lied To Their Girlfriends About Being Able To Cook And Now Have To Pull Something Out Of The Bag If They Want To Get Snogged." She did, however, have a chapter on poultry. I settled on a good old English dish that had apparently been Henry the Eighth's favourite – and look what a love life he had! Roast Chicken followed by Pizza. It sounded delicious.

"Happy?" asked Mum.

"A bit nervous, actually," I admitted.

"Nonsense," she said. "You'll be fine. You've got plenty of time after school to prepare it."

"Have I?"

"Are you sure you don't want me to help?"

"Positive," I said. Mum threw her arms round my neck and quivered with pleasure.

"You clever little Albert Roux!" she trembled. "And leave the defrosting of the chicken to me, all right? Now off you trot and get ready for school."

When I got to school, the playground was a hotbed of sexual intrigue. It was Bosie's rave that was doing it. Her secret love-fest devoted to endless carnal pleasure had triggered universal sighs of lust and longing. It was the nerve-tingling prospect of all those dark rooms and thick-pile rugs, the sensual combination of Hooch and hormones, the allure of unsupervised boy-girl bumper cars. Sharon and Darren were stroking each other's scalps. They'd both gone and got their heads shaved so they'd look like a pair of identical lovebirds, but I thought they looked like a pair of buttocks. Ginger was looking rather hot and bothered. Word had got out that he'd given me a judo lesson and there was a queue of girls lining up to grapple with him. Miranda Bletchley was at the front getting evil looks from the Flower twins behind her. Out on the mat, Ginger was getting really annoyed with Charlotte Sykes, who wasn't really interested in the judo at all. All Charlotte wanted was a demonstration of the folding press so she could lie on top of him.

"But that's wrestling," complained Ginger. "I do judo. There's a difference."

"So?" shrugged Charlotte. "I don't care." There were tears of frustration in Ginger's eyes, when he spotted me and asked for his guitar back so he could take it to the rave, but I told him I was having it dry-cleaned, which, for some extraordinary reason, he believed. Meanwhile Cecil, who, not surprisingly, had remained girlfriendless since Deborah's departure, was running up and down the queue asking if any of the other girls wanted to try him out for size while they were waiting, but none of them did. They didn't want to catch his eczema. Cecil promised to keep his jumper on with the sleeves pulled down over his elbows, but they weren't having it. Timothy and Alison sat smugly apart from the crowd and practised being married by not talking to each other, and Bosie kept pulling me into corners and telling me how much she was looking forward to the weekend. I pushed my luck a bit when I asked her for a warm-up kiss there and then, but she gently refused, and I was grateful that she did, because it proved to me that we had something deeper than all the other sad couples. We didn't need to indulge in vulgar displays of ritual courtship. We had a mutual bond of trust that transcended all that immature trouser fumbling and tasteless tonsil tickling. We had hands-off commitment, and you can't buy that by the pound at Asda.

On the way home from school, I popped into the Shop Here Please Shop to rent a video for after dinner. If it had been just for me I'd have chosen a video nasty or a horror film, but in Bosie's honour I went for something tender, something with a story and music and lots of Vaseline on the lens. Mr Patel recommended *Casablanca* and it cost £1.50 only.

"I'll give you fifty pence only," I said. "It's all I've got."

"Done," beamed Mr Patel. We had an understanding him and me.

"You're very cheery today," I observed.

"I am having the most wonderful news," he explained. "I am with woman. I am taking a lady out for a night on the tiles this weekend. My heart soars like a bald-headed eagle."

"Congratulations," I said. "What's she like?"

"How should I know?" he said. "We have exchanged details from the advert of hers that is all. But she sounds most suitable and has got a ready-made daughter!"

"One she made earlier, you mean?" I chuckled. "She's a "Blue Peter" presenter."

"What?"

I sensed his confusion and moved on. "Where are you taking her?"

"To the Taj Mahal," he declared.

"Isn't that a bit far away?"

"In Tooting. It is my cousin's restaurant.

They are very good at seducing the ladies between courses."

"Seducing?" I queried.

"With a violin, a sitar and a songbook of Ralph McTell hits."

"Oh, serenading!" I knew all about that.

"Yes. I am a big fan of "The Streets of London". I am so buzzing with excitement."

"I'm pleased," I said. "I'm entertaining a girl tonight as well, as it happens. Hence the vid."

"Good luck."

"I'm cooking."

"Then perhaps I should be wishing *her* good luck," chortled Mr Patel, his stomach wobbling at his own joke.

"Very good," I smiled. "Got to go."

"So the miniature turkey baster was not working then?" he said, just as I reached the door.

"What?"

"The spot in the middle of your chin. It did not remove it?" I felt my face to check he wasn't spooking me, and fingered a lump the size of one of Pongo's testicles.

I ran home like my trousers were on fire. Two and a half hours before Bosie came for dinner and God chucked this thunderbolt down on my head. So much for praying. How could He let this happen to me now, after all I'd done for Him? Why couldn't it wait till

Sunday to erupt? Why un-man me NOW?

When I ran into the kitchen, Mum was sitting at the table with her head in the sun lamp. She had a Piña Colada in one hand and a bottle of cooking oil in the other.

"Mum," I shouted, shaking with uncontrolled emotion. "There's been a catastrophe."

"Oh dear, pumpkin," she said, "never mind."

"No ... a catastrophe!" I repeated, thinking she couldn't have heard properly. "I wish I was dead!" But my subtle use of exaggeration fell on deaf ears.

"I'm just making myself beautiful," she chirruped, switching off the lamp and turning round. "How do I look?" Like a barbecued baboon in a bush fire, I thought. Her skin was scarlet and bubbling like molten toffee. She slipped off her sunglasses, revealing two white panda eyes, and gasped with pain as her lips stretched into a smile.

"You don't think you had it turned up too high?" asked Sherene as she came in looking for crisps. Mum didn't reply, just kept on smiling, which meant she was either waiting for a compliment or couldn't move in case she shed her skin. Then Sherene saw the spot and went into a big, witty routine, pulling yucky faces, making the sign of the cross with her fingers and chanting, "Unclean, unclean," like people do when they see lepers. "It'th the dreaded lurgie," yelled my cock-a-brained sister. "It's going to blow! Take cover!"

"It's only a spot!" I screamed.

"You could win firtht prize in a giant tuwnip competition with that." This was just what I didn't need. I expected my family to support me in my darkest hour.

"Tell her it's nothing," I growled at Mum.

"It's nothing, pumpkin."

"Don't lie!" I snapped. I wanted to hear the truth, but at the same time I didn't. My mind was in knots. I was a slave to my mental contradictions.

"All right, it's huge," said Mum. "And highly unattractive."

"You're a fine one to talk!" I exploded indignantly. Her sunburned face had cracked like a parched desert floor. I stormed upstairs and locked myself in the bathroom, but not before I'd passed Dad on the stairs.

"Did you know you've got a huge spot on your chin?" he said.

I assessed the damage in the bathroom mirror. The spot was a monster. It stared back at me like a bald goblin. "So what are you going to do now, lover boy?" it snickered. "Because I'm moving in!"

"I know what you're trying to do," I said. "I know you want me to squeeze you, so you can grow even bigger. Well, I won't!" What this boil had forgotten was that I was a spot veteran. I had a sign over my bed to prove it:

If I ever get another spot in my entire life, I
will never, never, NEVER touch it!
THIS IS OFFICIAL!

"I've got your number," I swaggered. "You can't wreck my life! I'm going downstairs now to cook chicken and pizza." I forced myself to look away from the mirror, but as I did so the chin goblin sneered at me.

"Do you really think Bosie wants to look at me all night?" it wheezed. The trouble with spots is they've got brains too. Evil ones, without compassion. If I ever wanted to wipe out the whole world, I'd just set loose a plague of spots and depress the human race into extinction. Anyway, the point was, I tried really hard to forget about my unwanted guest while I dressed for dinner, but IT wouldn't let me. It had infiltrated my brain like the Alien. Every time I moved or talked or thought, I felt it laughing at me. The plain fact was, I couldn't start cooking till I'd taught the little tyke who was boss!

I bared my teeth and growled at the enemy in the mirror. I prodded it gently from one side, then the other, but the subcutaneous network of roots bound my whole chin together and dispersed the pain through my jaw. This was a bubonic boil, it had to be. It was built like an iceberg, with only a third of its mass visible. I stretched back the skin on my chin with my fingers, turning the spot white and making it disappear. If only I could spend the evening like this, I thought, but how could I seduce Bosie with a couple of clothes pegs hitching up my chin skin? There was nothing else for it. One squeeze and it'd all be over.

I took a deep breath, leaned towards the mirror and applied sledgehammer pressure to either side of its base. Nothing. I squeezed harder and harder – the pain was piercing my temples like a tomahawk – and harder still! I had to stop before I broke my fingers. Now the unsquidged zit was scarlet and four times its original size. Maybe if I dug my fingers in underneath the pus sack ... gouts of salty water gushed out of my eyes. "Burst, damn you, burst!" I was pressing so hard my wrists locked into spasm. And then it happened. Like a rush of water through a hosepipe, I felt the pus move. A few seconds later it splattered over the mirror like venom from a spitting snake. My unbridled joy, however, was short-lived, because when I wiped away the blood, the extent of the damage became clear. I had blown a hole in my chin the size of a five pence piece. It was like looking down the shaft of a coal mine.

I beat my fists on the basin. Why did I never

learn? Tonight was supposed to have been an intimate dinner *à deux*, but now that my spot was larger than an average-sized twelve year old I'd have to lay an extra place, and as everyone knows, two's company, but three's a crowd. I hated Mum, I hated Dad, I hated Sherene, I hated the world, but worst of all I hated myself for being so weak-willed! Not only that, but time had mysteriously slipped through my fingers. The spot crisis had cost me hours. It was six o'clock. Bosie arrived in an hour and I hadn't started cooking yet.

Apart from a neck tourniquet, the only thing that was capable of staunching the river of blood gushing from my chin was a bath towel. Once I'd slowed the flow to a trickle, I camouflaged the volcano with a flesh-coloured plaster, knocked over Nan as she tottered down the loft ladder for dinner, and leapt down the stairs two at a time, towards the caterwauling that was Mum and Dad singing Elvis. They were standing in the kitchen like a couple of flamenco dancers – all frilly red lace and tight black suits. They were crooning "Love Me Tender", with a couple of large gin and tonics on the go.

"Haven't you gone yet?" I blurted out, terrified that they might still be here when Bosie arrived. The embarrassment of the three of them meeting was just too awful to contemplate.

"Cocktails at seven," said Dad. "Your mum and I are just having a pre-cocktail snifter before we go." He wrapped his arms round Mum's waist and drooled in her ear. "Love you, poodle!" he nibbled.

"Oh, God!" I muttered, as Nan came through the door and beamed gooily.

"The war's nearly over then?" she said. "It's good to have our menfolk home again, isn't it Babs?" I had to get rid of the lot of them.

"I've just heard the news. Apparently, the traffic's awful," I lied.

"You wouldn't be trying to get rid of us, would you?" winked Dad. "You wouldn't be embarrassed about Bosie meeting your old man, would you?"

"Don't be ridiculous!" I shouted over-defensively, causing Dad's eyebrows to shoot up in a knowing sort of way.

"Oh, Terry!" chided Mum, playfully. "You are awful. I don't know what's got into your dad these past few days. He's as frisky as a little bunny!" More like a randy old goat, I thought, as Dad patted Mum's bum and they giggled their way into the hall to put their coats on. Why can't parents just be normal, instead of veering from one embarrassing extreme to the other?

"Sherene's in the bath. Bed at eight o'clock."

"I know," I smiled.

"Have a lovely time," grinned Mum, kissing

me on the cheek and whispering in my ear, "the plaster's a big improvement."

"Thanks," I grimaced. Then under my breath, "Thanks for reminding me."

But before they could leave, the doorbell rang. It was Auntie Rene and Cousin Ramone, and Auntie Rene was wearing a sari. My eyes stood out on stalks.

"Er ... What are you doing here?" I floundered.

"You're babysitting me," squealed Ramone, flexing her "gumming" lips.

"I forgot to tell you, pumpkin," whispered Mum. "Auntie Rene's got a date tonight."

"In a sari?"

"She wants to make the right impression," Mum explained. "I don't expect you to understand, Johnny, but she needs a man." Mum's guilty look confirmed that I'd been set up. "She phoned and asked if you'd mind."

"Mind?" I could just see Bosie's face now. "But I can't babysit, it's illegal."

"Nonsense," chortled Mum. "You're fourteen." For once, I wished I wasn't.

"Look, this is serious."

"And you're being silly," said Mum, crossly, closing the discussion by ushering Ramone into the hall. Johnny Casanova was up Shit Creek without a paddle! It had never crossed my mind, not even in my worst nightmare, that I'd be sharing my first-ever intimate dinner with Nan Worms and The Naughties But Nicies!

The moment Mum and Dad had gone, I shot back into the kitchen to prepare dinner. I had forty-five minutes to get the food in the oven. Nan watched me quizzically as I turned the kitchen upside down looking for the chicken that Mum had promised to defrost. Imagine my horror then, when I opened the freezer and found that it was still inside.

"I don't believe it," I cried. "She's forgotten to do it."

"She's had a very busy day sunbathing," said Nan.

"Brilliant!" I bawled. "I'm dead!" There was no time to change menus now. I had to make the best of a lousy job. I dragged the pizza, the super-sized chicken and the half-opened packet of peas out of the freezer, and inspected the cooking instructions. The pizza took about twenty-five minutes at 220°C, but the chicken just said ROAST, which was about as much help as a white distress flag in a snow-storm. I remembered that Delia had said something about twenty minutes a pound and I figured it weighed two maybe three, so an hour max. would be plenty, even allowing for defrosting. I tore off its plastic wrapping, sat it in a baking tray, bunged it in the oven and turned up the heat to full blast.

I took the pizza out of its box, removed its

cling-wrap and put it on a smaller tray ready to go in in twenty minutes. I boiled a kettle and put the water into a pan, poured the peas on top and left them to simmer gently. I had a feeling something was missing. Potatoes. Of course! Mum always did spuds with chicken. I hunted through the vegetable rack, but all we had were two King Edwards with long green stalks sticking out of them. I couldn't make Bosie eat something that was still growing. I mean, I'd told her I could cook! I'd do a salad, instead. Unfortunately the cucumber had liquefied, the tomatoes were brown and wrinkly, and the lettuce was so limp it looked like the skin under Grandpa's chin just before he died. She'd have to make do with baked beans. I opened a can and put them on a low flame next to the peas. Then I hurriedly laid the table, shoved a white emergency candle into an egg cup as a centrepiece, two squares of kitchen roll for napkins and stepped back to admire my work.

"Is there a blackout?" wittered Nan, picking up the candle. "I didn't hear the air-raid siren." I took it out of her hand and put it back. "What's for tea?"

"You've already had it, Nan," I fibbed. "Don't you remember?" She looked puzzled.

"No."

"You should be in bed."

"But I don't go to bed till eight o'clock," she

said, sitting down. "With Sherene." The clock showed quarter to seven.

"Oh dear, the battery must be on the blink," I said, climbing on a chair and moving the hands forward to eight o'clock. "The clock's slow."

"Is it bedtime?" asked Nan.

"Yes," I nodded. "Night, night."

It took three minutes to push Nan up the stairs. I sat her on the loft ladder to catch her breath, while I whizzed back downstairs to put the pizza in the oven. On the way, I changed the other clocks in the house to eight o'clock so I could get The Naughties But Nicies off my hands. But just as I closed the oven, the front door slammed opened and Mum and Dad came back in. Dad's face was purple.

"The bloody car won't start!" he fumed.

"No!" I wailed. Hadn't I suffered enough? Of all the nights for the car to break down. Why did he have to buy a Lada?

"The battery's dead," he said.

"Oh," I squirmed. Now that *was* my fault. I hoped he wouldn't ask me if I knew anything about it.

"You don't know anything about it, do you, Johnny?" Why were parents so predictable?

"How could I?" I twitched. "I can't drive."

"Four and a half grand! That salesman's going to die for this!" he ranted. "We'll have to wait for a bloody cab now!"

"But you can't wait. That's not fair!" I cried. They both fixed me with a quizzical stare. "On you," I added. I had to get rid of them. "Look at the time!" I improvised, pointing at the hall clock which now said five past eight.

"Where did the time go?" puzzled Dad.

"You'd better hurry or you'll miss dinner," I pressed.

"He's right," panicked Mum.

"You'll have to run," I said.

"We'll have to run," copied Dad.

"But I've got heels on," whinnied Mum.

"Then take them off," I shrieked. "It's only a couple of miles." Thankfully, Dad and I were of a like mind, and in spite of Mum's complaints, he manhandled her out of the door like a bouncer. Meanwhile Nan had wandered back downstairs, complaining that she was still hungry. I told her she'd only get fat if she ate any more and shoved her back in the attic. On the way back down, Sherene and Ramone appeared from the bathroom with mascara moustaches painted on their top lips and a loofah and a loo brush hanging between their legs.

"We're men," they said.

"Bed," I ordered.

"But it'th not eight o'clock," Sherene stated defiantly.

"Oh yes it is," I smirked, rushing the two of them into Sherene's bedroom and pointing their noses at the doctored alarm clock. "It's five past. I'll tell Mum if you're not asleep in two minutes." Sherene scowled and stamped her foot, but I stood my ground and waited till they'd both climbed under Sherene's duvet. "Sweet dreams!" I warbled.

"Thour plumth!" she replied, as I slammed her door, took a deep breath, and rushed downstairs to turn all the clocks back to seven o'clock. The doorbell rang thirty seconds later. I switched out the lights, to hide my spot, and opened the door.

"What's happened to your chin?" asked Bosie.

"Cut myself shaving," I said quickly. "Lovely to see you, Mrs Cricket."

"I'll be back at ten o'clock sharp," said Bosie's mother, peering into the gloomy hall with a worried look on her face. "You're not on your own tonight, are you?"

"Oh no, Mum and Dad are out, but Nan's upstairs in the attic." She looked dubious.

"Show me," she said, protectively holding on to her daughter's shoulders so she couldn't come in.

"No problem," I replied through gritted teeth. "Wait there!" I couldn't believe it. I'd be fitter than Linford Christie after tonight. Nan was getting into bed when I burst up through the door in the floor. "Quick!" I shouted, "You've got to come downstairs."

"But it's bedtime," she said.

"No, no, in a minute. There's an air-raid. You've got to come."

"Into the cellar?" she asked.

"Yeah, you'll be safe down there."

"Lead the way," she giggled, swinging out of bed in her nightie. "Isn't this fun?"

"Sort of..." I sighed, as I steadied her down the ladder, helped her into the hall and presented her to Mrs Cricket. "See!" I said. "My Nan."

"Are you the ARP warden?" Nan enquired. "Shut the door! They'll see the lights and bomb us!"

"She's two pence short of a shilling," I whispered to Mrs Cricket.

"Yes, well, I'll see you at ten," she said nervously, backing away down the path. "Have a nice time, Bosie."

"Listen out for doodle-bugs!" called Nan, as I shut the door.

"I'll take her back to bed," I told Bosie. "Make yourself at home. Dinner's in five minutes."

"But it's too early for bed," stated Nan, pointing at the reset clock. "Look! Time's going backwards."

"Mr Churchill's orders," I said desperately. "To confuse the enemy."

"He's such a clever man," she said, allowing me to guide her back up the stairs to bye-byes.

It took ten minutes to get Nan settled. When I re-entered the kitchen, Bosie was sitting glum-faced at the table pointedly checking her watch.

"Sorry," I said, "I had to help her on with her gas mask."

"We've still got time," she said briskly. "We can just make it if we leave now."

"Make what?" I said.

"The Venue. The Deep Fat Friars are on."

"So?"

"So, I thought we could go and see them," she said, like I was a Classic Kevin for missing the obvious.

"I thought we were having dinner," I said.

"I told my mates we'd be there at seven-thirty, Johnny."

"But you didn't tell me. I've been cooking."

"Why would I be interested in food when there's a top-flight band on?"

"But I've been cooking."

"Dinner was just an excuse to get me out of the house, so my parents wouldn't suspect."

I was flabbergasted. "But I can't..." I bleated.

"Why not?" she jibed. "Where's your sense of adventure?"

"I'm babysitting," I said. "I've got The Naughties But Nicies upstairs." The corners of her mouth had drooped. "Besides, I've been cooking." I didn't feel she'd quite grasped the enormity of what I'd been doing.

"So you won't take me?" she said flatly.

"I can't," I muttered. "Sorry."

"Fine," she said, but it wasn't. The scowl on her face was regal. There was an awkward pause while I considered what I should do next, but I didn't see that I had any choice.

"Would you like anything to drink before dinner?"

"What have you got?" she said cheerlessly.

"Um Bongo or Ribena," I said.

"No wine?"

"No," I stammered. "Sorry. How about a peanut?" But she was allergic to nuts apparently. "Cheesy Wotsits?" I asked with my head buried inside the cupboard. "They look a bit stale, but if you eat them fast you probably won't notice." She wasn't interested. When I turned round from rummaging, she had a cigarette in her hands. She flicked her ash on the floor and studied me coldly. I think I was meant to be impressed. Then there was a second awkward pause which stretched longer and longer until I suddenly realized with horror that it was my job as host to keep things ticking over.

"So," I said light-heartedly. "How am I doing? Have I changed enough for you yet? Am I everything you've ever wanted in a man?"

"I'm fifteen," she said disdainfully, like I

was supposed to know what that meant, "and you're not. I have a woman's desires." My perfect evening had just gone pear-shaped.

"Shall we go through to eat?" I said, trying to keep it civil.

"Aren't we through already?" she replied frostily. I laughed to cover my gaffe, just as the door squeaked open and Ramone and Sherene jumped in with a fanfare.

"Ta-da!" they shrieked. "We're both Supermodels!" They'd got Mum's high heel shoes on and were wearing their knickers over their pyjamas. They pretended to fly round the table singing "SuperMODELS!!!" at the top of their voices until Sherene got tired and flopped down into Bosie's lap.

"Do you wear a bra?" she asked, staring deep into Bosie's eyes.

"Get out of here! Now!" I bellowed. "This is private."

"We knew you had a girl down here," she continued, mischievously. "Do you want to thee Johnny with no clotheth on?" Ramone plonked a large, red photo album on to the table. "We've got hundredth of pictureth in here of Johnny with hith willy hanging out, or have you already theen it?" Ramone sniggered at her cousin's daring display of wit. That was when I went tonto and span out of control like a circular saw in a twister. I chased them out of the kitchen with bloodcurdling threats of what I'd do to them if I caught them.

"Get upstairs, or I'll put spiders in your bed and tell a murderer where to find you." It did the trick. They fell over each other with terror and locked themselves into Sherene's bedroom. I could still hear them screaming ten minutes later. Bosie, however, was not amused.

"That wasn't very p.c." she said, when I returned. "They're only children."

"You don't have to live with them," I told her.

"You should be ashamed," she said, in a voice that reminded me of Mum's when she was telling me off. "You said you liked kids."

"Sorry," I said for the umpteenth time, although I didn't know why. Bosie's eyes flicked away from mine and never properly looked back all night. "I'll get the food then," I said. "Don't get up!"

"I wasn't going to," she said.

"I can manage," which was the stupidest lie I'd ever told, because when I opened the oven I hadn't a clue what to do first. I put on one of Mum's old oven gloves and pulled out the charred remains of the pizza, clattering the tray on to the floor as it burned my fingers. The pizza bounced and rolled across the lino, hitting a chair leg and spinning to rest topping-side down. "That was hot!" I jested.

"What is it?" she asked.

"Pizza," I said. "Don't you recognize it?" I picked it up off the floor, plonked it in the middle of the table and turned my attention to the chicken. It didn't look like Mum's normally did. It was pale and white, like a bloodless finger, and was sitting in a shallow pool of water. "Do you prefer breast or leg?" I asked, but Bosie couldn't answer. She was tasting the hairy pizza.

"It's just like cardboard," she spluttered, spitting a mouthful of half-masticated biscuit over the table.

"It shouldn't be," I said, turning over the base to see what the problem was and discovering a cardboard plate underneath. I think I was meant to have removed it before cooking. I snorted nervously and hurriedly tossed the pizza into the bin like an iron Frisbee. "God! Honestly, this oven! It's been playing up for weeks! There's plenty of chicken, though."

Unfortunately there wasn't plenty of chicken, because when I tried to carve it, the knife bent as if made of rubber. I prodded the flesh with the fork, but even the prongs wouldn't go through. The chicken was as hard as a paving slab.

"You did remember to defrost it, didn't you?" asked Bosie, watching me struggle with the brick-like bird.

"Yeah," I lied, thinking Mum was dead meat when I got hold of her. "There must be something inside, that's all. Maybe it's still full of eggs." Bosie sighed terminally. She was wearing her disappointment like a wide-brimmed hat. I stuck my hand up the chicken's bum and felt the end of a plastic bag. "Here's the problem," I announced, withdrawing a sack of raw giblets. "I forgot to take its guts out." But their removal made no difference. The chicken was still a solid block of ice. I didn't know what to do. The sweat was rolling down my arms and dripping off my wrists.

"I thought you said you could cook," she said accusingly.

"I can ... normally," I gibbered.

"Just like you can *normally* manage to work out at the gym and get yourself a tattoo?" she said. There was real venom in her voice.

"Can you pass me a bucket?" I said urgently. The carcass was gushing gallons of pink, tepid water and the baking tray was overflowing. Bosie leaned behind her and handed me a blue bucket, into which I emptied the tray. It was Pongo's bucket. The one he wore over his head. The one without a bottom. The chicken juice sloshed on to the lino like a mini-waterfall and splashed up Bosie's tights. She screamed and leapt off her chair.

"Well, it's not my fault," I wailed. "You passed it to me!"

"They're ruined," she yelled. "They cost a fortune."

"I'll buy you a new pair," I crawled. "Have you ever thought of becoming a vegetarian?"

"Why?"

"Because I've got some peas and beans if you're still hungry." But the peas had dissolved into pea soup and the baked beans were burned black. "How about a coffee, then?" I asked, but Bosie had lost her appetite and was looking at the door like she was getting ready to go.

ON CATERING

No wonder all the famous cooks
Are mad and bad and grumpy.
It's 'cause the cooking takes so long,
They don't get rumpy-pumpy.

(Johnny Casanova – hanging up his meat cleaver for good)

"Let's just chat," I suggested pathetically, adding in desperation, "I'm looking forward to the rave tomorrow, aren't you?" I didn't know if I dared mention the kiss, but I had cooked her dinner so she did owe me. "I can't wait to do it."

"Is that all you ever think about?" she sniffed. "Sex?"

"No," I protested. "No. It's being with you that's the thrill. A kiss would be nice, but it's not essential."

"Good," she said, "because I never do anything I don't want to. Like stick with a boy who doesn't do what I ask, for example." This was followed by an egg-on-face silence, during which I must have checked the knots on my shoelaces at least twelve times. Why was she acting so differently now that we were alone? It was like she was deliberately pushing me away, like I was such a tragic disappointment to her that she didn't want me any more. It was like she hated me and wanted me to hate her, and, truth be known, her behaviour was having the desired effect. I kept telling myself I loved her, but I couldn't remember why. All I could think was that Ginger didn't have to do anything to impress his girlfriends, so why did I? Bosie wouldn't even give me a kiss, and I'd changed every little bit of me to keep her happy. I didn't know what else to do!

Just then Pongo let rip under the table. Bosie wrinkled her nose with disgust. I booted him in the belly to make him stop, but my kick seemed to work in reverse. A green cloud wafted out of his rotting tubes and I had to drag him outside before Bosie suffocated.

"So, you also lied about being kind to pets," she jabbed.

"Yeah, but he just farted," I explained. "He's got to be taught a lesson."

"I disagree," said Bosie. "Cruelty is cruelty

whichever way you dress it up." Her unfounded criticism stung me to the quick.

"Look, I'm only trying to make things nice for you," I said weakly.

"Well, it's not working!" said Bosie. "I'm going to phone my mum."

Before I could stop her, Nan appeared in her gas mask, weeping hysterically, saying she could smell burning and had we called the fire brigade. By the time I'd got Nan back into bed and raced back down from the attic, Bosie was standing in the hall in her coat.

"I'm going," she said. I didn't want to stop her.

"Sorry the food wasn't edible," I muttered. "See you tomorrow?"

"Seven o'clock," she said. "To help with the furniture." Then she opened the door and disappeared into the night, attitude and all.

"Well, she might have said thank you," I mumbled miserably to Pongo. He whined and cocked his head on one side. "Yeah, and I love you too, mate."

ON UNDERSTATEMENTS OF FACT

An Understatement
Would be thus,
That I'm not
Bothered by my pus.
Another one might

Run like this,
That Bosie likes
To take the piss.

(Johnny Casanova – why does the course of true luv refuse to run smoothly?)

The more I thought about the dinner, the more depressed I became. Maybe I *should* have abandoned Sherene and Ramone and gone to The Venue, but there again, maybe Bosie should have had the wit to notice what an effort I'd made on her behalf. I wandered out into the garden to share my loneliness with the stars. Something told me Bosie didn't like me any more; that I was too young for her or something, that I'd let her down, or maybe she'd found someone else. Whatever the reason, I was slowly realizing that the less she liked me, the less I liked her. Still, it wasn't all doom and gloom. Both of us still had something the other wanted. She wanted someone to help move the furniture and I wanted a snog. It wasn't so unreasonable. I mean, I was fourteen years old, and time was creeping on. I could be bald in a week and then who'd want to kiss me? I had to grasp Bosie's offer now, while I still had my own hair, and if that meant stringing her along for the duration of the rave, then so be it. Love, I was rapidly discovering, was the first cousin to war.

There was a light on in Sam's window, and Sam was flicking twenty-foot V-signs at me, via the shadows on our wall.

"I saw Bosie leave early. What happened?"

"If you've got three weeks, I'll tell you about it."

"Be right down," shouted Sam, who was never one to pass up a juicy piece of gossip. "Did you do it?"

"No," I said, as we flopped down on to the sofa. "The Second World War kept coming between us! Want to watch a video?"

"What is it?"

"*Casablanca*," I said.

"Sounds boring," said Sam.

"Yeah, but the trailers might be good," I said. But they weren't. They were trailers for old films, the sort of films that made our parents cry.

"There's some frozen chicken left over if you're hungry," I offered.

"Yum, yum!" snorted Sam. "Is it really, *really* cold?"

"As a penguin's nuts," I said, which had us laughing for about five minutes, till Sam said, "I wonder if penguins' nuts are dry-roasted or just plain salty?" which kept us giggling till the film started, by which time we were so exhausted, we couldn't move.

"This is nice," I said.

"Very comfortable," said Sam.

"Are you coming to Bosie's rave tomorrow?" I asked.

"Probably."

"Come with me."

"It's easier if I make my own way. In case I change my mind."

"Fair enough," I shrugged.

"But thanks for offering," said Sam. The film *was* boring. Tonnes of kissing and slushy music. Hardly a gun in sight. *And* it was in black-and-white. I felt my eyes closing.

"How do you chuck someone, Sam?" I asked, through a blissful mist of half-sleep.

"Never done it," yawned Sam.

"I'm going to wait till after she's snogged me."

"Good idea. Never pass up a snog."

Now I was yawning too. "Thing is," I mumbled, "she doesn't really like me. I've tried to be everything she wants me to be, but it doesn't seem to work."

"You should try being yourself," said Sam. "That's about the only thing our mums and dads *have* taught us."

"It seems to work for Ginger," I smiled.

"Yeah," said Sam sleepily.

"Yeah," I echoed. "Good old Ginge." Then my eyes slammed shut and my head rolled off the cushion.

When Mum and Dad came back an hour

later, they found me and Sam asleep on the sofa with the film still on. I had my mouth wide open and was snoring, and she had her head in my lap and wasn't.

13
DREAM ON

That night I had the weirdest dream.

There I am, megaphone in hand, standing on the pitch at Wembley Stadium. My words are flashed up on the scoreboard, each one twenty foot high, so that every man Jack of the seventy-thousand crowd can read them. Bosie is suspended above me in a fishing net. A camera feeds a fifty-foot image of her face to a video screen at the other end of the stadium. And I'm tub-thumping like a preacher.

"You and me," I'm hollering, "we're history, babe." The crowd roars, egging me on. "You've done nothing but criticize me since the start." Another roar. On the screen, a vast, whale of a tear rolls down Bosie's cheek and drips off her chin on to the grass. "I drink tears for breakfast, doll. Turn off the tap! You don't move me no more!" And the crowd's going

berserk, and the Queen's applauding, wearing a pair of Dame Edna specs, and she's waiting to give me the cup, but first I've got to boot Bosie into outer space. So I strap on my inflatable Converse One Stars and whack her through the clouds, and on the screen Bosie's screaming, but nobody can hear her words, just read them.

"I'm sorry, Johnny. I love you. Take me back!"

But I'm the mean machine, the Casanova Kid, I'm the Three-K Cutie (kosset 'em, kiss 'em and kick 'em out!) and frankly my dear, I don't give a damn!

But then the Queen gets the hump, puts on a black cap, points at me and says, "You's going down, Casanova!" And down I go, into the bowels of the earth, where it's hot and steamy and Sherene's kissing David Hasselhof on a surfboard, and Pongo's keeping the fire burning with his gastric gases, like a living set of bellows. I'm in Hell. They're all down here. Mum melting her face by the flames and rubbing in suntan cream, Dad wiring up Mr Driver's gonads to a car battery, and Ginger with his clothes in shreds, being chased by six thousand ugly girls and begging them to leave him alone (I like this one). Up above, the angel Bosie flutters her wings and looks smug and calls me a clueless nerd who's gone where he deserves, but I can't say I'm sorry, because I don't feel it. So I blow her a raspberry while an arrow sings through the smoke and pierces the tattoo on Bosie's heart. I spin round to see who's shot it, and there's a faceless woman dressed in a black leather jerkin with tights underneath and a pair of legs like she's on stilts. They go past her armpits up to her ears.

"I've been looking for you everywhere," she says. "Do you want to dance?" And next thing I know we're grooving, swirling round in a psychedelic shower of metal petals, and everyone's jealous, because I'm the undisputed Hardcore Dance King of the world and she's the Golden Queen, the snogtastic Betty in tight trousers, the hottie with the curly black hair.

And then I woke up, more confused than ever.

TREE OF TRUTH

Throw me a line, I'm drowning.
Tell me we both feel the same.
Is the tree where I'm barking
Not worth the parking?
Should I bark up a trunk new of name?

(Johnny Casanova – stumped)

14
THE RAVE

The next morning, my emotional nerve endings were raw. It was no longer a question of should I chuck Bosie, but when and how? A letter was too business-like, a fax too public, a phone call too impersonal. It had to be face to face at the rave that night, but what was I meant to say? How can you be kind and cruel at the same time? This is what I came up with.

"Surprise! We're finished." But it seemed a trifle heartless. I thought again. "Bosie, we've got to talk." That was a good start. She'd know from the no-nonsense tone of my voice that something serious was coming so she'd be prepared and wouldn't faint. "Recently, I've found myself strangely attracted to Bird's Eye Dinners for One." Brilliant! But what if she followed my meaning to the letter, jumped the gun and verbally abused me? I'd have to beat her to it. "You're wasted on me, Bosie. I'm a no-good, low-life bum. You deserve richer pickings." What better than lashings of self-loathing to take the wind out of her sails and buy me time to hit her with the big one? "We both know it's not working." Now that it was out in the open she'd probably start crying, so I'd dollop on the sympathy to soften the blow. "Of course there'll be tears and sleepless nights, maybe even a suicide attempt or two, but it'll be kinder to both of us in the end." She'd get angry at that. "You hate me now, but you'll thank me later." I had to look to the future, paint with broad strokes of optimism and humour. "There are plenty of other fish in the sea. Look at that hunk over there. He's got more muscles than a whelk stall!" Reassure her that she was still beautiful. "I'll always love you—" But not so beautiful that I wanted her back— "like a sister." And then, if she still hadn't got the message. "I hate you. Get lost!" That should do it. A swift, clean break, leaving me free to sow my seeds elsewhere. But I still couldn't help feeling sorry for Bosie. Rejection, however sweetly packaged, was always a bitter pill to swallow.

Ginger phoned after lunch to ask for his guitar back for the rave and I had to do a pretty nifty side-swerve to put him off the scent.

"It's cleaned up a treat," I told him. "I'll bring it with me." Actually it wasn't so much a side-swerve as a whopping great lie, but it got him off my back. I hadn't intended to tell Ginger about the big bust up, it being a private affair between Bosie and I, but you know how it is when you've got news and it takes control of your mouth muscle. He was my best mate after all.

"I'm chucking Bosie tonight, as it happens," I said casually.

"Really?" he replied. He didn't sound as surprised as I thought he might. "I'd heard she was dumping you."

"What?"

"I met Sharon and Darren in Safeway's. They said."

"Oh bums," I panicked. "Whatever you do don't tell Bosie what I'm going to do, because then she'll dump me first and I'll be the one who gets hurt."

To add to my woes, at about three o'clock the front doorbell rang. Mum and Dad had disappeared into their bedroom for a little siesta so I had to answer. It was Auntie Rene, still wearing her sari, and carrying a newspaper under her arm.

"Is your mum in?" she asked.

"They're in bed," I said. "Shall I get her?"

"I think she'd want to hear my news," she beamed, pushing straight past me and skipping into the kitchen. Mum and Dad shot out of their bedroom like startled rabbits when I knocked on the door and rushed downstairs in a fluster. They didn't look like they'd been sleeping at all.

"I'm not stopping," Auntie Rene announced breathlessly. "I said I'd deliver your paper to help Mr Patel out."

"Have you not been home?" asked Mum. Auntie Rene blushed.

"Oh, Babs," she gushed. "He's perfect. Tonnes of money, his own business and always the perfect gentleman. Ramone and I will never want for anything again."

"Except brains," I muttered.

"What do you mean?" enquired Mum, while Dad readjusted his dressing-gown.

"I asked him to marry me," beamed Auntie Rene. Mum's face was a picture.

"Shouldn't you get to know him first?"

"Mr Patel was your date!" I interrupted in amazement. I'd just worked it out.

"Isn't it wonderful?" crooned Auntie Rene. "We're moving in next weekend."

"Does Mr Patel know?" asked Mum.

"He said he'd think about it," said Auntie Rene quickly, "but I'm sure he won't object. Anyway, must fly. Got to dust off my curry cookbooks." And off she went, spinning out of the house with her daughter, like a passing tornado that had stopped briefly to mess up our lives.

It was now four o'clock and I was due at

Bosie's at seven. The fact that halfway through the rave I was suddenly going to be girlfriendless influenced the way I dressed. At some point in the evening I was going to be single again, available to hunt or be hunted. Accordingly I had to look safe and snogtastic. The tousled hair with casually romantic fringe said *Pulp*, so the clothes had to match. I didn't actually possess any authentic Geek-Chic gear, but a quick flick through Dad's wardrobe produced a corking pair of Terylene slacks with stay-press creases, a wide-collared purple shirt, a floral kipper tie, a snazzy sports jacket from Harry Fenton and a pair of easy-clean shoes with elasticated laces – "wipe once with a damp cloth and see them shine!" The mirror confirmed what I already knew. *You're hot to trot,* it told me. *You're sex on legs!*

I was downstairs ready to go by six-thirty. Sherene sniffed deeply as I walked into the kitchen.

"Phwaw!" she gasped. "You thmell like a whore'th drawerth!"

"Sherene!" rebuked Mum. "Language. I think you smell very fresh, pumpkin."

"Thanks," I said. It was a subtle blend of CK One, Dad's aftershave, Mum's deodorant, minty toothpaste, mouthwash, Lynx body spray for men, Gold Spot breath freshener and athlete's foot powder, which I'd tipped liberally down my socks. All body odours were firmly under wraps for the night. I wasn't taking any chances. I was hermetically sealed.

"And you look so pretty, pumpkin, just like your father," she smiled. "Come and give Mummy a kissy."

"Mum!" I whined, pulling a face like she'd just asked me to do the washing up.

"Don't be stupid, pumpkin. You may think you're a man, but to me you'll always be my sweet baby boy." I hung limply in her arms, like a rag doll, while she pressed me to her bosom. "There now, that didn't hurt did it?"

"Do you want a lift?" asked Dad. Everyone was being so nice. It was most unsettling.

"No, I'll walk," I was going to say, but he'd already got the car keys out. "Only if you drop me round the corner," I said. Dad smiled like he'd just recognized himself in me or something.

"I do love you, son," he whispered. "It's all right. I understand. You walk."

"Thanks," I said. I had to get out of there before he burst into tears.

Something made me look up. I was outside Mr Patel's shop. It was boarded up and had a handwritten notice hanging in the window which said: *To all my customers. Have gone on an extended holiday. Don't know when I shall be returning. Happy Christmas. Mr Patel*

That's strange, I thought. He never closes. I wonder why? A furtive figure emerged from a side door with a battered suitcase in his hand. "Mr Patel," I called out, making him jump out of his skin. As I ran over he searched the street nervously for an escape route, but I had him trapped against the wall. "Where are you going?"

"Most urgent business in India," he replied, keeping his eyes on the pavement.

"When will you be back?"

"Hard to say," he said, looking up slowly to study my reaction.

"This wouldn't have anything to do with Auntie Rene, would it?" His eyes flitted from side to side, like two bluebottles trapped in double glazing.

"Don't be taking this wrongly," he whispered. "She is a most honourable lady, Johnny, but she did scare the pre-nuptial pants off me last night. I am now more certain than ever that I'm happier single."

"So you're running away?"

"Not in so many words, but yes," he said. "Please don't be telling her where I have gone, and make my most humblest apologies, but I am too cowardly for her."

"Between you and me," I said, "I think you're making the right decision."

"Thank you," said Mr Patel, with a note of relief in his voice. "Now I must be rushing if I am not to miss my plane. Goodbye." He started to go, but turned back suddenly and shook my hand. "My blessings on you, Johnny Casanova. It is a warm cockle day to have been seeing you before I leave. Namaste." Then he bowed and scuttled down the road, casting furtive glances over his shoulder lest Auntie Rene should be lying in wait to pounce on him with a wedding ring. Mr Patel's decision to give up his dream of married bliss, by leaving Auntie Rene, confirmed what I already knew: that I was doing exactly the right thing by dumping Bosie.

It was starting to get dark as I strolled up the front path to Bosie's house, and as all the lights were off I couldn't find the doorbell. I thought I'd found it on the right-hand side of the door, but when I pressed it nothing happened, so I gave it a tug and it came away in my hand. It wasn't a bell-pull at all, it was like a small wooden pencil case with brass ends. It had funny squiggly writing all over it and a little window halfway up. The door opened and Mr Cricket peered down at me.

"Sorry," I grinned, sheepishly, handing him the cylinder. "I don't know my own strength." He didn't look too pleased.

"Evidently," he glowered. "You're meant to touch it, not wrench it off the wall." At first I didn't recognize Bosie, standing just behind her father. Her hair was pulled back off her face and trapped beneath an Alice band of dark blue velvet. She was wearing one of those sensible Laura Ashley-type dresses, made of winceyette pyjama material with a frilly, white lace collar. It made her look years younger.

"What is it?" I whispered to her, as her dad hung the cylinder back on its nail.

"A mezuzah," she said.

"Bless you!" I quipped, but the joke fell flat.

"Shut up!" Bosie hissed nervously in my ear. "Pretend you know what it is."

"This is Michael," said Mrs Cricket, introducing me to Bosie's younger brother, who was dressed up real posh in a suit and tie with a tiny little cap on top of his head and a white tea towel round his shoulders.

"Hello," I said. "Been having your hair cut for the bar mitzvah party?" Michael looked embarrassed.

"It's my tallith and kippa," he said.

"Tallith and what?" I replied, as Mr Cricket closed the front door with a sharp push. "Is that some sort of fish?" Bosie grabbed my arm and shoved me into the cloakroom, while her mother and father watched me strangely.

"I've told them you're Jewish," she gabbled.

"What? Why?"

"Because I am," she squealed, "and so's my brother."

"Congratulations," I said. "So?"

"Try to look like you know what's going on. My parents think I'm having four friends round for dinner and they've only let you come because I've told them you're a nice Jewish boy."

"I thought you said they were liberal with a small 'l'."

"I lied," she hissed.

Well, what a surprise, I thought.

I followed Bosie into the sitting room, where her parents were standing with their coats on.

"Now that you're here, Johnny, we can go," said Mrs Cricket. Her father stepped forward and stared me right in the eye.

"Don't watch too much television. Don't touch the drinks cabinet. Don't go upstairs. Don't eat the matzo balls and don't fiddle with the stripped lulav."

I wanted to ask him where I was supposed to have a pee if I wasn't allowed in the lulav, but I didn't want to make him any more tense than he already was. So I said instead, "Oh, have you got the decorators in?" by way of making polite conversation. "Stripping the loo lav wallpaper, I mean." Bosie laughed nervously.

"Johnny's always making jokes, Daddy. He's pretending he doesn't know that a lulav are branches we strip for Shavuoth."

"Are you sure you're Jewish?" snarled Mr Cricket.

"Oh definitely," I winced. "I've had my thingummy done and everything."

"Hadn't you better be going, Mummy?" said Bosie all of a sudden, with a pained look on her face.

"I think we should," replied her mother.

"We won't be back till late," added Mr Cricket. "Don't forget the washing up."

"And do enjoy yourself," added Mrs Cricket, kissing her daughter on the cheek. "Shalom, Johnny."

"Shalom," I said. Then everyone repeated the word over and over, so I did too. I said it to everyone, including their cat, who'd come in to see what all the noise was about. As they left the room, I sensed that Mr Cricket didn't trust me. He gave me a stern look, like he thought I was the son of Beelzebub creeping in to steal their daughter's soul. On a scale of good to bad, the impression I had made on the Crickets was burned toast and bombing.

When I finally plucked up the courage to speak to Bosie, my voice was squeaking like a mouse in a mincer.

"Sorry," I said. "You should have warned me."

"I thought you'd be intelligent enough to guess," she snapped. "Let's move the furniture." We shunted sofas and carried chairs in silence. I kept looking at Bosie, hoping she'd be able to read my mind. If we could get the kiss over with before the rave, I could chuck her before everyone arrived and then I might enjoy myself. On the other hand, I didn't want a row. She looked fierce enough to make chopped liver out of me. So I said nothing, but kept my lips available just in case she felt like using them. She didn't.

After we'd raided the drinks cabinet, removed half the light bulbs and put newspaper on the floor to save the carpet, Bosie went upstairs to change. She came back down wearing a tiny white leather skirt, which was so short that I was told to turn my back while she hopped down the stairs, and a tight T-shirt that was held together at the sides with red laces, so that most of her body was showing. She'd let her hair down and was hobbling about on a pair of high-heeled shoes that ruled out proper walking in case she fell over. She tottered to the door as people arrived with cans of beer and cheap bottles of cider, and went into frivolous hostess mode, whirling her arms around her head and shrieking like a howler monkey in a poor imitation of somebody enjoying themselves. I didn't see her again for at least half an hour, by which time the joint was jumping.

It was like a snake pit. Wild jungle music pounded the walls and throbbed like the shock waves from an H-bomb. Bodies thrashed in the dark. Legs stuck out of sofas, arms waved behind doors and tongues were so frantically busy that I couldn't work out where the burble was coming from. I mean, there was so much kissing going on that nobody had the time to talk. Not me, though. Bosie was giving me a wide berth, leaving rooms when I came in, turning her head away when I tried to catch her eye, pretending she had something burning in the oven when I managed to get close. There was an atmosphere between us you could have cut with a knife. It didn't go unnoticed either. Sharon and Darren had obviously been commandeered to keep me away from her and were shadowing my every move.

"What's the matter with you?" snarled Sharon. "Why are you upsetting Bosie?"

"I haven't done anything," I shouted to make myself heard over the music. "I haven't touched her."

"Not through lack of trying," bellowed Darren.

"What do you mean?"

"She's told us all about you," screamed Sharon. "All about your wandering hands and silver tongue. We've heard how she's had to fight you off. You're an animal. You should be put down!"

"She told you that?" I gasped. "That's a lie."

"Calling her a liar now are you?" postured Darren. Maybe I should have been scared, but I couldn't take him seriously, not looking like a refugee from a boys' band, in his tight jeans and blouson shirt slashed to the waist so his nipples showed.

"No," I said. "I don't lie, Darren, but you do, every time you're with Sharon." He didn't know what I meant and neither did she. I wasn't too sure myself, to be honest, but it sounded dead clever. On that high note, I took my leave of Bosie's bewildered bodyguards and went in search of Ginger, who I'd seen coming in a couple of minutes earlier.

It wasn't difficult to find him. Where there was girls, there was Ginger. He was like the Pied Piper of Hamelin. He was standing on the kitchen table performing an Osaekomiwaza to an audience of twenty. They were lapping it up, applauding his every grunt and laughing loudly when he fell on his back and waggled his legs in the air. As I pushed my way through the crush, I accidently bumped into Timothy and Alison and knocked a glass of orange juice out of her hand. Timothy gave me the evil eye, but it wasn't my fault that they were standing in the corridor like a pair of middle-aged parents, the only two people at the rave not dancing or snogging (apart from me, obviously).

Ginger jumped down off the table when he saw me in the doorway, grabbed a can of beer and came over.

"Have you done it?" he asked.

"What?"

"Chucked her."

"No. I can't get near her. There's too many people."

"Well, cheer up," he said. "You look like the sky just fell on your head. This is a party." I knew that, and I really wanted to have a good time, but I just couldn't.

"So much for getting snogged," I moped. Ginger nodded in the direction of the girls in the kitchen.

"I could lend you one if you want," he grinned. "Talking of which – lending, I mean – have you got it?" The question caught me on the hop.

"Got what?" I replied.

"The guitar."

"Oh that," I gulped. "Sorry, mate, but I forgot." He looked me straight in the eye.

"That's the third excuse you've made," he said. "You've broken it, haven't you?" It was destined to be a night of truthfulness.

"Only a little bit," I protested. "It wasn't what you'd call a big explosion." What you'd call a big explosion was what Ginger then did to my bread basket. "I thought T'ai Chi was supposed to teach you inner calm and self-control," I gasped.

"That was a rabbit punch," he seethed, his eyes inflamed with wrath.

"It was an accident, mate," I explained. "I didn't throw the bucket of water. I'll make you another."

"*Make* me another?"

"From an old tortoise shell," I improvised.

"Well, that's a bit of luck, isn't it?" he sneered sarcastically. "Because I just happen to have an old tortoise shell on me. Perhaps I should write to "Blue Peter" for a pattern."

"Good idea," I said, but Ginger wasn't joking.

"I want a new one," he said. Then he walked away and came back again, like a dog worrying a bone. "And, by the way, I bet I know just what's under that plaster – the biggest and most disgusting eruption ever!"

Up until then I'd been really calm about the spot. I'd avoided all mirrors and reflective surfaces in case a sighting plunged me into a whirlpool of depression. I hadn't peeped or prodded it or stretched my face to see if it had gone. But now that Ginger had reminded me it was a record-breaker, I couldn't think of anything else. It felt like a living, breathing bowling ball. I was seriously thinking about leaving early when Sharon poked me in the back. She had something to say and nothing was going to stop her.

"You might not like Darren and me," she said, "but we don't care, because the feeling's mutual. I just wanted you to know that Bosie doesn't like you either. She thinks you're a cheap fake!" I was piqued.

"It doesn't bother me," I lied, hurting like

hell, "because I don't fancy Bosie any more."

"Oh, that's nice," she said. "A real gentleman you are, Johnny. I'm going to tell her." Now I'd blown it.

"I'd rather you didn't," I said, but she'd already shot off. I would have gone after her, but I was mown down by Cecil, who'd been drinking copious amounts of lemonade shandy and was obviously starting to feel sexy. He swayed into the kitchen, lurched over to Daisy and shook her hand.

"Hello, Rosie. I'm Cecil," he announced. "Do you like me?"

"I'm not Rosie," stated the look-alike, coldly. "I'm Daisy."

"Will you dance with me?" he asked. Daisy looked to Rosie for help. "Hello, Daisy," said Cecil at once. "How about you? Do you like me?"

"It's Rosie!" barked the twin. "Go away. I'm with Ginger." Cecil's little face fell into his name-tagged socks and his mouth collapsed like the cut-out smile on a rotting Hallowe'en pumpkin.

"But I like you," he blubbed. "Both."

"Oh come on, Cecil," comforted Ginger. "There are plenty of other girls here." But the shandy had transformed Cecil into the Incredible Sulk. He was out of his shell and wanted revenge.

"I'll get you," he muttered under his breath.

Daisy and Rosie mocked him by pretending to be scared. "No more Mr Nice Guy," he yelped. "You lot are crisp bread ... I mean, toast!" Then he tossed back his head and marched upstairs with a look of fierce indignation behind his spectacles.

Had the whole world gone mad? It certainly went a bit flaky when I saw Sharon collar Bosie by the hi-fi and whisper something sneaky into her ear. Bosie shot me a venomous look, which made my blood run cold. She knew. Sharon had told her. Self-preservation was my only thought. I realized instantly that the kiss was history, that the only way forward was to dump Bosie before she could dump me. If anyone was going to get hurt, it was her. My stomach turned somersaults as I ran through my plan of action. A quick strike, in and out like the SAS, with as much of my self-esteem intact as I could manage.

I cornered her in the sitting room and backed her up against the shelf containing her Mum's collection of china dolls.

"Hi," I said.

"I'd like a word," she interrupted coldly, stopping me dead in my tracks. "A real word." It was the way she said "real" that made my bowels freeze. She *was* going to chuck me, wasn't she? That wasn't in the script. She couldn't. She wouldn't! She would! She was pulling a face like she'd sucked on a lemon. I had to move like lightning to avoid a public humiliation.

"I'd like a real word too," I said feebly. If she really was going to finish it, I'd race her to the post. "I don't think it's working," I said.

"What isn't?" she queried. "Us?"

"Yeah," I said.

"Neither do I," she said with unfeeling precision. I had a horrible feeling that the axe was just about to fall. My stomach clenched, my palms sweated, my eyelids twitched, and I blurted out the first thing that came into my head to stave off the inevitable death-blow.

"Do you want to dance?"

"Look, I don't want you to take this the wrong way..." she said.

"Oh, but I will," I gabbled. I was falling to pieces.

"But—"

"I know what you're going to say," I interrupted. I had to speak the cruel words first. Breaking up had to be my idea!

"But I don't want to go out with you any more," she said, in a doom-laden voice that bomb-blasted my brain and paralysed my senses. Damn her, she'd won!

"That's not fair," I moaned, as a feeling of empty despair overwhelmed me.

"But you wanted to finish too," she said defensively, and suddenly I realized that if I played the injured party, I had all the power. I could make her feel awful just by acting gutted. For the first time in our relationship I could make her do what I wanted. I was in charge.

"No, I didn't," I said. "I was going to ask you to marry me, but it's all academic now."

"Don't be ridiculous," she laughed.

"Oh, I'm ridiculous now, am I?" I said. "Thanks. Remind me to wear a red nose next time I'm with you."

"People split up all the time," she said angrily. The guilt was starting to bite.

"Then I won't be lonely on the scrap heap, will I?" I said, sniffling back a crocodile tear. "I hope you're satisfied. You take someone's life, Bosie, turn it upside down, squeeze it for all you can get out of it, then chuck it away like a used rag. I hope you can sleep tonight." This was better than a snog. I felt so powerful. "And I never wanted to kiss you anyway." I only slipped this in as an aside, but it proved to be a big mistake, because it made her cry. Now, instead of being in control, I was fumbling around begging her to stop. The dancing had stopped. The lights had been turned on. People were staring at us. Sharon, Darren and Timothy to name but three, and the one with the sloping forehead was still looking for an excuse to pay me back for nicking his trunks. With nostrils flaring, he stormed over and shoved me into the drinks trolley, which tipped over under my weight and showered my hair with warm cider.

"You made Bosie cry!" he thundered. "Nobody makes the hostess cry! Got it?"

"Actually, I'm all right now," Bosie interjected unexpectedly. She'd turned off the waterworks and was smiling triumphantly. So *she* hadn't been crying either. Those had been crocodile tears like mine. What was happening to us? The gloves were off. We were both playing games to try and make the other feel worse. I understood then that love and hate could be two sides of the same coin.

LUV AND HATE

I bought a bunch of grapes
With a coin of solid luv,
But the change that I got back
Was in hate...
And the grapes went bad.

(Johnny Casanova – paying dearly
for falling in luv)

"I wouldn't cry over you, Johnny Worms," jeered Bosie, "if you were the last man on Earth!" Crueller and crueller. How had this mutual separation spun so horribly out of control?

There was a commotion at the door.

"Let me through," shouted a girl's voice. My heart gave a tiny, involuntary leap, like the first flutter of a fledgling's wings. And that was before I'd even seen who it was. I just knew. It was Sam. She pushed her way through the crowd and stood behind Bosie with her hands on her hips. I felt weak and light-headed. She looked stunning in her black leather trousers and studded jacket. She tapped Bosie on the arm. "Leave him alone," she said. "You've had your fun, Bosie. Now move aside!" I was gobsmacked. She was standing up for ME! Bosie shoved Sam's shoulder and forced her mouth into Sam's face.

"You're welcome to the moron!" she sneered, at which insult Sam shoved Bosie back. A buzz went through the rave. The music was switched off. The dancers cleared back against the walls leaving a space in the middle of the room. It was like being in a Western. Bosie struck first, grabbing a fistful of Sam's hair and tugging her head back. Sam just laughed.

"You've asked for it now," she said, grabbing Bosie's wrist and squeezing till Bosie loosened her grip. Then she twisted Bosie's arm up behind her back until our hostess dropped to her knees and begged for mercy. Unfortunately, that was when Sharon weighed in on Bosie's side.

"Leave my best friend alone!" she roared,

charging Sam from behind. As Sam fell forward, she tumbled into Timothy who tripped over me. Sam was back on her feet in a crack, her eyes flashing as she squared up to Bosie and Sharon with her fists clenched.

"Sam, stop!" I screamed from underneath Timothy's sweating bulk.

I jabbed him where the sun don't shine and rolled him off me. "Stop it, all of you!" A full-blown cat fight had started up. Bosie was pulling Sam's ears, while Sam was flailing her fists like lump hammers at Sharon who was lashing out with her sling-backs and crying out for Darren to help her, but he wasn't getting his nipples tweaked for anybody. That was when I noticed that Timothy had got back on his feet and was swinging for me.

"Duck!" shouted Ginger, sliding across the newspaper and sweeping Timothy's legs from under him before he could mash my nose.

"Respect!" I grinned at my best mate. He was having fun.

"I couldn't leave you to get pummelled," he whooped, as Alison, joining the fray to protect her fiancé, shoulder-charged Ginger like a linebacker. Ginger toppled sideways into Darren, who'd been stung into action by Sharon shouting that she wouldn't love him any more unless he got stuck in. Anyway, he didn't get the chance, because Ginger's weight threw him off balance and he accidentally head-butted Timothy who was trying to rugby tackle me from the side. Their two skulls met with a sickening crunch of thick bone. I called to Ginger to pull me out from under their unconscious bodies, but he was saving Sam from a double duffing up from Sharon and Bosie. Unfortunately, Ginger playing Sir Galahad with Sam stirred a jealous giant in the breasts of Rosie and Daisy, who piled into their rival like a twin-headed missile, and knocked her out of Ginger's arms. The arrival of the Flower twins opened the floodgates. The rest of Ginger's harem, fearing lest they should lose Brownie points for not coming to his rescue, joined in too. Sadly, however, not against Bosie's mob, but against each other. Sensing that this was their chance to see off the competition, they piled into a ruck and rolled around the floor like maggots in a bucket. Up until then, Cecil had been cowering on the sofa, but the sight of so many girls twisting and turning at his feet inflamed his manly passion.

"I love you all," he shouted as he jumped on top. "Who will be my girlfriend?" Unfortunately, in the struggle his shirt sleeves got pushed up and his eczema exposed. It was Charlotte Sykes who got scraped with it first. She screamed and caused a chain reaction which twisted the maul inside out as the girls all turned their fury on Cecil. It was mass hysteria. Cecil was bawling his eyes out as I struggled out from underneath Timothy and Darren and shuffled slap bang into Bosie.

"I hate you!" she wailed, delivering a stinging slap to my right cheek.

"And I hate you, because she hates you!" added Sharon, turning my other cheek towards her and slapping that too. Unfortunately, the force of her fingers ripped the plaster from my chin. The fighting ceased abruptly as the rioters gawped at my seeping spot. Their silent staring eyes completed my misery. I had to get out of there! It was Ginger who gave me the opportunity to do so. Bursting through the crowd like Bruce Lee, he scythed a path towards the French windows, seoinaging, ogoshing and limb-lashing everyone in sight.

"I told you Judo was useful," he cried, as Bosie cartwheeled towards him and knocked him out with a spinning stiletto.

I stumbled over the chaos of bodies and fell through the French windows into the garden. "So much for love!" I mumbled bitterly as the door closed on the fighting. My heart was as heavy as a bag of dough. My dreams for the rave had come to nothing. Changing myself to meet Bosie's specifications had got me nowhere. I was taking myself off the market. No more girlfriends. It was strictly shower catalogues from now on. I slid down the patio wall and sighed deeply like a corpse in a morgue. "Bums, bums, bums, bums, bums, bums, bums," I groaned, dropping my foolish head into my hands.

WHAT'S INSIDE?

Pain and hollow emptiness,
Does my leaden soul possess.
Deeper down there's only more,
I'm rotten to my lifeless core.

(Johnny Casanova – prisoner of the bleak Now never-ending)

Someone shuffled in the shadows on the lawn.

"Who's there?" I asked. Sam stepped forward into the light.

"I came to find you," she muttered.

"Are you hurt?"

"Only scratches. What are you doing out here?"

"Licking my wounds," I said. Sam cocked her head quizzically to one side and moved closer. "I had so much to offer, but Bosie didn't want any of it." I glanced up and smiled pathetically. She looked so unbelievably beautiful that suddenly I remembered what *I* looked like. "Sorry," I winced, covering my chin. "This spot's revolting." She put her hand up to stop me talking.

"I wasn't looking at it," she said, in a voice

that dripped warm honey down my spine.

"But I'm not perfect," I mumbled as her nose brushed across my skin.

"Who wants perfect?" she whispered. "I like you just the way you are." Her lips sent a tingle to my toes as they caressed mine and suddenly I didn't want to be anywhere in the world but there, in that garden, at that precise moment, with Sam. Why I hadn't noticed her before I shall never know. I was in Heaven. Then we clocked out of worldly time and shared a sweet, shivering sensation of seismic dimensions by kissing our necks off.

THE KISS

Waiting,
Wanting,
Breathing,
Brushing,
Blowing both our minds away.
Sweetness,
Softness,
Wetness,
Oneness,
Let us make it last all day.

(Johnny Casanova – 'nuff said)

15
THE MORNING AFTER

It wasn't just an ordinary kiss. Kissing Sam made me forget who I was and why I'd been so miserable half an hour before. It was like a magic, healing cream that soothed the rawness of reality. It was like dreaming. It was like drowning in liquid fudge. It was like ... like I'd always imagined love would be.

When we walked back indoors, Bosie was clearing up as fast as she could. Her parents were due back any minute and it looked like a bulldozer had run wild through the house. I think Sam and I must've been radiating something pretty horny, because everyone stopped rushing and stared at us like we were VIPs, like we were Bruce Willis and Demi Moore or something. But we weren't trying to be – we were just us, and I didn't care what other people thought. I was as high as a kite and kept laughing. We parted the crowd in the hallway, a bit like Moses and his Mrs paddling through the Red Sea, and came face to face with Bosie at the door.

"Goodbye, Bosie," I said calmly. "Sam and I are leaving." She stared at me in a way I'd never seen before, like suddenly now that I didn't want her any more, I was worth having. Then her nose wrinkled at the sides and she started to cry.

"Get out!" she screamed, kicking a pile of beer cans like a spoiled child. "Get out all of you!" Luckily, we did as we were told, because seconds later, Mr and Mrs Cricket screeched to a halt in front of their rave-damaged house and Bosie fainted.

Sam and I walked home under the clouds.

"Are you my girlfriend, then?" I asked boldly.

"I hope so," she chuckled. "But it's taken you long enough to ask."

"I'll make it up to you," I said. "Are you free tomorrow morning?"

"My place. Nine o'clock," she replied.

"I'll be there at eight-thirty," I said, pulling her into a bush and kissing her long and hard till it thundered. I wanted that moment to go on for ever. But then it rained, and we got soaked to the skin, so it didn't.

The next day I woke up feeling awful. I had a raging headache, a runny nose and a fit of non-stop sneezing. I refused to let it blight my sense of joy, however, and bounced out of bed, threw on the first thing that came to hand (no more image-conscious dressing for me now that Sam loved me for myself), and skipped outside to greet the beautiful day.

Sam was waiting for me when I rang on her doorbell.

"What's the matter?" I asked, concerned, as she opened the door. Her eyes and nose were red and puffy. She looked like she'd been crying.

"I've got the flu or something," she said. "It came on last night before I went to sleep."

"Do you still want to go out?" I asked, rubbing her shoulder. She smiled.

"What do you think?"

"I think you're gorgeous," I whispered, which made her giggle and sneeze at the same time.

We walked down the road hand in hand. I was proud to be seen with her. I wanted to show her off to all the passers-by, especially when one of them was Ginger. He came limping towards us with two black eyes and a plaster across the bridge of his nose. When I was sure he was looking at us, I leaned across and gave Sam a kiss on the cheek.

"You don't mind me doing that, do you?" I checked.

"No..." she mumbled, scrunching up her nose and sneezing. "I like it."

"Good," I said, wiping the tears from my eyes. "Hi, Ginge."

"Hello," he said warily, sussing out the situation. "Are you two ... er...?"

"It happened last night," I grinned.

"So why are you crying? He hasn't dumped you already, has he?"

"Flu," Sam told him.

"And what happened to you?"

"Bosie!" he said painfully. "You never told me she was a black belt."

"You never asked."

"Never again," said Ginger bitterly. "Girls are trouble! I'm going home to bed." And he dragged his broken body round the corner, while Sam and I headed for the bus stop.

The bus was half-empty. We went upstairs and sat at the front. I put my arm round Sam's shoulder and she snuggled her head into my neck. It wasn't at all embarrassing. Unfortunately, this coincided with a violent attack of sneezing, which carried on for several minutes, shook Sam off the seat, and left me shivering and shaking like a Chihuahua at the North Pole.

"There's something not right here," I said, as Sam's eyes flooded with salty water and her nose ran freely down her top lip. "I mean, flu doesn't strike this quickly, does it?"

"I don't feel up to going out," she admitted.

"No, me neither." We were both sniffling and snuffling so loudly that people were moving away from us on the bus.

"You don't think we caught something serious last night, do you?" she asked.

"Like what?" I wondered, wiping my nose on my sleeve.

"Well, I don't know. Some sort of rare kissing disease!" We stared at each other open-mouthed as the bus pulled up at a stop.

"Where are we going?" shouted Sam, as I dragged her down a short cut.

"I know a doctor," I said. "She's a bit mad, but we can't afford to hang around if it's a rare disease."

"But it's Sunday," protested Sam.

"It's an emergency," I assured her. There were several doorbells to choose from when we arrived at the surgery, so I pressed the lot and shouted, "Let us in!" A bleary voice on the intercom asked us what we wanted.

"Help!" I said. The door buzzed and we ducked inside to be greeted by the doctor in her dressing-gown. Her badger-streaked hair was sticking out like a bird's nest.

"You!" she yawned. "I might have guessed."

"No, it's important this time," I insisted. "I've done with puberty. This is life and death."

"It will be if you've got me out of bed for

nothing," growled the doctor. "Who's this?"

"Sam," I said. "My girlfriend. We're in love."

"Congratulations," mumbled the doctor. "Is that what you've come to tell me?"

"No. Look, I know this is going to sound stupid—" The doctor laughed.

"Amaze me," she said.

"But I think we may have caught a rare kissing disease."

"It's true," said Sam.

"Come through," said the jaded doctor, opening the door to her surgery. "Now what are the symptoms?" She listened distractedly as we told her about the sneezing and runny noses and watering eyes and headaches.

"So what do you think?" I asked fearfully.

"I think I might know what the problem is," she said, consulting a large medical tome on her desk, entitled *Rare and Fatal Diseases*. "Have you been caught in a rainstorm recently?"

"Last night," said Sam.

"Oh, God, please don't let it be fatal as well," I whimpered, "because I love her, you see, doctor. She's the only girl I've ever cared about. She likes me how I am. I don't have to pretend I'm something different with Sam." My voice trailed off into a squeak as the doctor tapped a page dramatically and sat back in her chair.

"I think I've found it," she said grimly.

"What? What is it? Tell us the worst!"

"It's not fatal," she smiled reassuringly. "You're not going to die." I grasped Sam's hand and squeezed it tightly.

"Thank heavens," we beamed together.

"But you are, I'm afraid, allergic to each other."

"I beg your pardon?" Sam's face had turned white.

"Your house mites are incompatible," explained the doctor, "and, well, unfortunately there's only one cure..." We held our breath. "No touching, no holding hands and no kissing," she said. "Ever."

"Please!" I gasped. "PLEASE! TELL ME IT'S A JOKE!"

"It's a joke," said the doctor. "You've both got colds."

I told you, didn't I? I hate doctors!

JOHNNY CASANOVA
THE UNSTOPPABLE SEX MACHINE

Jamie Rix

Johnny Worms is hot to trot, the unstoppable sex machine, Johnny Casanova.

Well, so he believes. His best friend, Ginger, may tell him that "girls is trouble", but when love's thunderbolt strikes in the form of Alison Mallinson or a beautiful vision in purple, what can Johnny do? Is it his fault he's irresistible?

"Genuinely funny … sparklingly well-written." *The Independent*

"Hilariously funny." *The Times*

THE FIRE IN HENRY HOOTER

Jamie Rix

Everyone knows to fight fire with fire. But how do you fight a fire demon?

When Henry Hooter's parents are killed in a freak accident at the Light Fantastic Firework Factory, eleven-year-old Henry is left alone with some burning questions. Like why is the fiery-tempered new owner of the factory so interested in the Howling Hullabaloo Howitzer, the last rocket invented by Henry's parents? Where have the town's children started disappearing to? And are there really such things as dragons and fire lakes? As the answers emerge and sparks begin to fly, Henry wonders whether he's got himself involved in something that's just too hot to handle.

Find out why in this explosive book by the award-winning author of *Johnny Casanova, The Unstoppable Sex Machine*.

STORMBREAKER

Anthony Horowitz

Meet Alex Rider, the reluctant teenage spy.

When his guardian dies in suspicious circumstances, fourteen-year-old Alex Rider finds his world turned upside down.

Within days he's gone from schoolboy to superspy. Forcibly recruited into MI6, Alex has to take part in gruelling SAS training exercises. Then, armed with his own special set of secret gadgets, he's off on his first mission.

His destination is the depths of Cornwall, where Middle-Eastern multi-millionaire Herod Sayle is producing his state-of-the-art Stormbreaker computers. Sayle's offered to give one free to every school in the country – but MI6 think there's more to the gift than meets the eye.

Only Alex can find out the truth. But time is running out and Alex soon finds himself in mortal danger. It looks as if his first assignment may well be his last...

Explosive, thrilling, action-packed, *Stormbreaker* reveals Anthony Horowitz at his brilliant best.

"Suspenseful and exciting." *Books for Keeps*

"The perfect hero ... genuine 21st century stuff." *The Daily Telegraph*

POINT BLANC

Anthony Horowitz

Alex Rider, teenage superspy, is back!

Fourteen-year-old Alex Rider, reluctant MI6 spy, is back at school trying to adapt to his new double life ... and to double homework.

But MI6 have other plans for him.

Investigations into the "accidental" deaths of two of the world's most powerful men have revealed just one link. Both had a son attending Point Blanc Academy – an exclusive school for rebellious rich kids, run by the sinister Dr Grief and set high on an isolated mountain peak in the French Alps.

Armed only with a false ID and a new collection of brilliantly disguised gadgets, Alex must infiltrate the academy as a pupil and establish the truth about what is really happening there. Can he alert the world to what he discovers before it is too late?

THIRSTY

M.T. Anderson

"When you get thirsty, you get angry without reason. Increasingly. You feel prone to violence. You feel prone to drink blood..."

Chris just wants to be a normal guy – to hang out with his friends Tom and Jerk, avoid his bickering parents, get a date with Rebecca Schwartz. Lately, though, he's had this strange, abnormal desire, a thirst for blood... He needs help – but who can he trust? Chet, the oddly cynical celestial being? His friends? His family? Can he even trust himself? Time is running out and Chris is *so* thirsty...

"A dark, witty story with a twisting, turning plot."
The School Librarian

MISTER SPACEMAN

Lesley Howarth

Thomas Moon is a space freak. His room's done up like the Mir Space Station. He hunts the websites daily for space news and stories. He wants to be an astronaut. And according to the mysterious e-mail he's just received, addressed to Mister Spaceman, his dreams are about to come true...

"Each of her books is an invigorating display of verbal fireworks, and a fresh foray into the imagination." *Gillian Cross, TES*

LOST IN AFRICA

Nick Warburton

Tramping through the African jungle is not Natasha's idea of fun.

But her civil-servant father, Ronnie Banham, has had a row with his boss and decided to leave his home at "the Station" in the African state of Liberation. On Christmas Eve, with an old pram full of possessions and their passports in a rucksack, Ronnie, Natasha and her little brother Colin set out on foot into the unknown, where mangrove swamps, crocodiles, war and many other hazards await them...

"A superb, gripping novel." *Tony Bradman, The Daily Telegraph*

RIDING THE WAVES

Theresa Tomlinson

"Don't let the waves frighten you. They can knock you down, but they can't stop you getting up and trying again."

When Matt goes to visit old Florrie as part of a school history project he doesn't expect to enjoy himself. He'd much rather be down on the beach with the young surfers he hero-worships, riding the waves – if only he had a board. There's a lot more to Florrie, though, than meets the eye, and her personal history has some uncanny similarities to Matt's own...

Commended for the Carnegie Medal

"Sparkling, moving and funny." *The Guardian*